BAYOU REVELATIONS

THE CRANE DIARIES 6

BY APRYL BAKER

BAYOU REVELATIONS

Limitless Publishing, LLC
Kailua, HI 96734
www.limitlesspublishing.com

Formatting: Book Pages By Design
Cover Design: Deranged Doctor Design

ISBN-13: 978-1-64034-807-3

DEDICATION

For April Dawn Kilpatrick
You've helped me more than you know
when it comes to writing this particular
book, and you got me back on track with
my storytelling.
Thank you.

Saidie Walker

Jacob's Fork, WV

"Saidie, this is Dad. Your mom and I have discussed it, and we think it's best you don't come to your brother's birthday party. If you want to drop off a present for him, that's fine. Hope you're doing well. Talk soon."

The voicemail replays over and over in my head.

A broken record.

But I guess that's me…broken.

Some days are harder than others, like

today. It's my brother's birthday, but they don't want me to come to his party. Mom can't bear to look at me most days. My dad's getting better, but they apparently don't want me near my little brother. They're afraid the family curse will rub off on him or something.

Necromancy.

A curse and a blessing.

Ever since I woke up with my dead dog lying next to me in bed, this power I inherited from my great-grandmother has caused every single problem in my life. From losing my family to coming into contact with a Necromancer who tried to kill me for my powers. Being a Necromancer pretty much sucks.

"Knock-knock!"

The apartment door opens, and Alex sticks her head in. We all have keys to each other's student apartments in case of emergency. And in our crazy supernatural world, emergencies are a dime a dozen.

Dark blue eyes narrow as soon as she sees me. "What's wrong?"

I motion to the answering machine,

unable to even say it. It hurts too much.

Curious, Alex goes over and hits play. I watch her face morph into righteous indignation. "They can't do that!"

"They can." I pull my knees up and wrap my arms around them. "They're his parents, and it's their house."

"That's not fair."

"No, but what can I do?"

Alex comes over and plops down beside me, her black hair flying out behind her in all directions. It's a lot longer than it used to be. As heavy as her hair is, I'm shocked she doesn't always have a headache.

"Why don't we go to his school at lunch and you can give him his present there?"

"Because then Mom would get pissed and take me off his authorized pickup list. What if there's an emergency and I'm the only one available to get him? If I'm not on that list, it doesn't matter who I am. He's stuck."

"Would your mom really do that?"

"She would." My mother is a deputy sheriff. The school would ask no questions about the change because she's a police officer.

"I'm so sorry, Saidie."

She looks as miserable as I feel. "Can you take his present over to Mom's for me? I don't think I can face either of my parents."

"I thought your dad was coming around?"

I laugh, the sound hollow and bitter. "He's going to do whatever Mom tells him to do since she's the resident expert on the family curse."

"I wish I could fix this for you."

Alexandria Reed is the kindest person I've ever met, despite everything she's been through. She's also the reason my Necromancy woke up. When she came home, her own magic called out to the people she needed to make her whole, to help protect her, and that meant me. I blamed her for a long time, but we've moved past that. She's my best friend…no, she's more like my sister now. I don't know what I'd do without her.

Alex reaches out to hug me, and her

hands fall away. Her magic and mine don't mix well. I almost killed her last time she touched me. She has the ability to absorb others' gifts, and being around Aleric, my boyfriend and Luka's brother, she cloned his vampirism, for lack of a better description. When I touch her, I accidentally drown her in death magic. That doesn't happen when I touch Aleric. It's something we're still trying to figure out.

"Has your mom made any headway on why my magic tries to kill you?"

Alex twists her hands, one of her tells that she's nervous. "No. She even reached out to her contacts in Europe. No one can explain this."

"Well, damn."

"Pretty much."

"When are the boys supposed to be back?"

"I got a text from Aleric at four in the morning saying they'd be gone all day. Who would have ever thought four-wheeling on the Hatfield-McCoy Trail would turn a bunch of grown men stupid? What the appeal is to getting covered in dirt and dust is beyond me."

"I know. Jason even sat down and had a discussion with Luka on the best brands of helmets, and you know my brother stays as far away from Luka as he can."

Alex's brother is slightly terrified of her boyfriend. Then again, Luka's Gypsy magic gives him dominion over the shifters. He can make them do whatever he wants. Not that he does, but I wouldn't put it past him to do so if it was necessary to keep Alex safe.

"Maybe helmets is the equivalent of shoes to guys?" Alex tries to keep a straight face but fails. She and I both burst out laughing. The two of us had tried to talk shoes to the guys once. It was like we were speaking a foreign language.

There's a knock at the door, and I frown. Bree, my roommate, is out of town with her family, and all the guys are gone four-wheeling.

"You expecting someone?" Alex stands, and I can see her wolf shift behind her eyes. She inhales and leans toward the door. Her expression clears almost instantly. "It's Uncle Sabien."

Sabien Blackburne has sort of become the pseudo-uncle for all of us. When Alex opens the door, he doesn't look surprised to see her here. The two of us are nearly inseparable. Sabien and Alex look alike, whereas Jason looks like his father, John Reed. Jason does share the Blackburne eyes, though. Deep, deep blue, but when they get upset, they swirl with a color that's not quite identifiable.

Aleric tells me my eyes remind him of storm clouds. They're just plain old gray to me.

"Alex, I was hoping you'd be here." Sabien closes the door behind him and walks into the room, his complete attention settling on me.

He doesn't look happy.

"I got a call from New Orleans."

My entire body tenses, and memories assault me. Memories of the crazy Necromancer who almost killed me and of her swamp creatures. It was the single most horrifying moment of my life and one I will never forget. I have nightmares almost every single night.

"It was about the island."

"No…she's dead."

"But her creatures aren't." Sabien comes and sits beside me. "I told you we'd have to deal with this eventually. When you killed her, all her magic went into you, and those creatures became yours. Even the vampires."

"Kristoff…the dreams."

"You've been dreaming of him?" Sabien tries not to sound alarmed but fails.

I nod. "Yeah, he's been playing a starring role in my nightmare."

"It has to be related."

"To what?" Alex asks.

"To the phone call I received from Robert Willow. One of their hunters was taken by Kristoff, but they were able to retrieve her. To get to him, they have to go through Madame's security measures, and for that, they need a Necromancer."

"I can't…" I shoot up off the couch and retreat to the kitchen. "I can't go back there."

"Saidie, everything that belonged to Madame now belongs to you. That's the way it works in the magical community. Even if those creatures weren't your responsibility, there's not another Necromancer close enough to deal with everything."

"Please don't ask me to go back there."

"Hey, you're not going by yourself. We'll all go with you."

"It's too dangerous." I can't put her in that kind of danger, not after everything she's survived. She's still half convinced she's crazy and living in her own dream world. Who knows what that place might do to her psyche?

"All the more reason you need us. Uncle Sabien's right, though. We can't let those things hurt people if we can stop it."

She's right, and I know it, but that doesn't make this any easier.

"When do they need me?"

"Today."

Today? They want me there today? I...

Alex gives me a reassuring smile. "It's okay, Saidie. I'll make sure it's all okay. We'll do this together."

I nod. I don't want to go, but if the

dreams I've had of Kristof torturing and murdering girls weren't just dreams, I can't sit here and do nothing. I have to stop him.

"I'll make the travel arrangements."

"All of us, Uncle Sabien, even Jason and Conner."

Sabien agrees and leaves.

New Orleans, here we come.

Emma Crane

New Orleans, Louisiana

"Sit still."

"No. It itches."

Mary lets out a long sigh. "Em, I swear if you don't stop moving, I am going to stick you with this safety pin."

"I don't know why I even agreed to this." I glance over at my grandmother, who is happily talking away to some of her friends. She looks ecstatic, whereas I look as miserable as I feel. "It's not like we've even set a date yet."

"You know Lila. She wants to get a

jump on things." Mary hums as she works on the third wedding dress I've tried on. "How do you like this one?"

"I don't. It's too much fluff."

"You're supposed to have fluff on your wedding day." Mary looks exasperated, but I'm irritated.

"Says who?"

"Says me. You know I'm not going to put you in anything that looks ridiculous."

My arm starts to tingle, and I rub at it absently. It's the arm Kristoff broke. Silas healed it, but it tends to ache from time to time. Not sure if that's just me remembering the threat Kristoff poses. He scares me. It isn't the fact that he's a vampire or that he has super strength. It's the look in his eyes. He has dead eyes, a serial killer's eyes. He's evil through and through.

"Aren't we supposed to meet those people from West Virginia today?"

Mary shakes her head. "No, they don't get here until tomorrow. You're stuck here with your grandmother until she decides to set you free."

"Well, dang."

Mary snorts, a habit she picked up from me.

Lila looks up and smiles. Of course she'd love the dress that looks like some kind of fairy tale princess with big puffy sleeves and a hooped skirt. How you'd even sit down in this thing, I don't know.

My grandmother is a force of nature, and she always gets what she wants, but she and I are gonna fight if she wants me to wear this dress.

She gets up and comes to stand by Mary. "You look beautiful, Emma."

"I look like a Disney princess gone wrong. I'm too short for this dress. It's made for someone who's at least six inches taller."

Before Lila can argue, Mary steps in. "She's right. With her height and body style, this dress doesn't do anything for her."

Lila's lips thin. "It's such a beautiful dress."

"Agreed, but not for Em. She needs something simpler, more classy. Let me look around, check out some indie designers I've had my eye on. We might even have one made specifically for her."

"That's not a bad idea." Lila's look becomes calculating. "You find the right designer, and I'll take care of the cost."

"Guys, I thought the bride had some say in all this?"

Mary and Lila both give me a look that says, "Who told you that?"

"We might as well call it a day here. I don't think this shop is going to offer anything we need."

"She's only tried on three," Lila argues.

"But I've looked through everything while she was in the dressing room. There's nothing here I'd dress her in."

"I'm not five," I mutter. "I can dress myself."

They ignore me again, and I give up. I stomp back to the dressing room and work for a good five minutes to get out of the dress. Lord only knows how much this thing costs. If I tear it, Lila buys it, and as upset as I am right now about having to do this, I'm careful. Money gives me hives.

When I come back out, they're chatting with some of Lila's friends. One of them has a granddaughter getting married, and the young lady in question looks happy as can be to be trying on gowns. Sometimes I wish I could be the granddaughter Lila deserves, but I'm me, and I'm done regretting I'll never be who she wishes I was. Even if she won't admit to herself how she really feels.

But really, the reason I'm so resistant to the idea of dress shopping is because I miss my mom. I want her here with me to find the dress that makes me shine and feel like a bride. Every girl wants their mom there while planning a wedding, and as tomboyish as I am, even I feel like that. And I'll never have it, so I will never be excited about this.

"I'm ready to go," I announce as I come up beside Mary, and my stomach growls. It's been hours since breakfast.

"Your stomach's ready to go," Lila corrects me with a smile. "Your father's stomach still rules his schedule, too."

"How is Ezekiel?" The youngest of the women looks up expectantly. Probably the bride's mother. She looks about Zeke's age, but she has on too much makeup. I can tell because of how the lines around her eyes look like dried-up riverbanks. Mary's practiced her makeup tutorials for her channel enough that I've picked up a few things. It's hard not to when she does it in front of me for hours at a time.

"He's doing well, Virginia. Thank you for asking."

"Doug was saying just the other day we all need to get together and have dinner. With my daughter and your granddaughter getting married, we can compare wedding plan notes."

My face blanches. I don't even need to be in front of a mirror to tell. I can feel the color leach out of it. Have dinner with high society people? Talk wedding plans all night with a bride who seems like a little kid with a sugar high running from one dress rack to another? *Please, no*.

"That sounds wonderful, dear." Lila beams at her. "I'll talk to Ezekiel about an evening when he's not busy and call you."

"I can't wait."

No one notices how sickly I feel except for Mary. She takes my hand and guides me away from the happy people. "It's okay. It won't be that bad. I'll be there to help." She knows how much I dread parties. I'm not good with people. Well, rich people, anyway.

"Why does she do this to me?" I whisper once we're outside the shop. "She knows I hate parties."

"She's excited, Em. You're her only grandchild, and you're getting married. She missed out on everything with you growing up, like birthday parties, school dances, prom. She might be overcompensating a little because of that. Let her have her fun. It makes her happy to be able to do this for you."

"And I'll do it for you as well, Mary, when you find your special young man."

We both jump at the sound of Lila's voice. She's snuck up on us. It's a trait she and Zeke share. They're quieter than church mice. I keep asking them to teach me, and they just stare at me like I'm crazy.

"Emma may be my only grandchild by blood, but you and Eric are ours as well. All three of you mean the world to Josiah and me. We are as much your grandparents as Emma's, and we love you."

Mary looks dumbstruck. She spent her whole life growing up without grandparents, and when her dad died, it was just her and her mom. Mrs. Cross spent a lot of time working, so Mary was by herself a lot. Me and Eric being family was one thing, but I know how much she loves Lila, and hearing Lila call her their grandchild, I think it did my sister in. Mary and I aren't related by blood, but that doesn't matter. She's the sister of my heart and, apparently, the granddaughter of Lila's heart as well.

"You know that, don't you, Mary?" Lila looks as dumbstruck as my sister, who tears up. She hugs Mary tight. "Josiah and I love you as much as we do Emma, you and Eric both. We'd adopt you if we thought your parents would let us so you could have the same last name as us."

Mary's mom would freak out if they ever asked her that, and Lila knows it, but telling Mary is entirely different.

"I love you, too," Mary whispers, choked up.

"I love you, too, *Grandmère*," Lila corrects her. "I've told you to call me grandmother on more than one occasion."

"I love you too, *Grandmère*."

"There's my girl." Lila gives her another quick hug. "Now, ladies, where do you want to eat lunch?"

If it were up to me and Mary, we'd eat somewhere with good burgers, but not Lila. She never eats at a burger place.

"Wherever is fine, as long as they have food I recognize."

Lila shakes her head ruefully. I will never have her refined palate. "How about that little Irish place that just opened off Bourbon? I hear they have delicious shepherd's pie."

"What's that?" Mary and I ask together then laugh.

"Do you know what fish and chips is?"

We nod. Everyone knows what that is. "Then you know they have something you'll eat. Your grandfather and I spent two years in Ireland, and we both love the food. It's time for my girls to start getting exposed to things besides burgers and fries. You need to learn to feed my grandchildren."

"Uh, you realize I'm not even married yet, and Mary still has to find her future husband? Kids are way, way, way down the road for us both."

Lila smiles that mischievous smile. It's my smile, so I know it well. "All the best plans change, sweetheart. You may find yourself a mother younger than you think."

Nope. Nope. Nope. Dan and I talked about this. We both have too much going on right now to even think about kids. It's why I got an IUD. No slip-ups.

Besides, I'm terrified of being a mother. I haven't had the best of role models. Claire, as much as she loved me, was a heroin addict and didn't make the right motherly choices. It's not like I've had anyone to really look up to either except Mary's mom, and I wasn't in her care more than a few months. I'd probably kill the kid by accident.

And I'm too young. I'm still in college, for Pete's sake.

Just talking about having babies gives me hives.

O'Ryan's Pub was so far off a place where I'd expect to find my grandmother eating that it isn't even funny. The place is cool as heck with its Irish decor and signs showcasing their large selection of beer. I mean, really, it's an Irish pub, and the one thing the Irish are known for is drinking. Secretly, I think they invented St. Patrick's Day as another excuse to drink.

We slide into a booth near the back, the rich leather upholstery one more thing to love. The lights look like those Tiffany lampshades with colored glass.

Our server, Sean—pronounced *Shawn,* as he informs us—speaks with an authentic Irish brogue and is as charming as all Irishmen are reputed to be. He winks at Mary, who blushes three shades of pink.

"What the heck is bangers and mash?" The menu might as well have been in a foreign language, for all I recognized the dishes.

"Sausages and mashed potatoes." Lila grins when Mary and I both make a very disgusted face. I'm not opposed to breakfast sausage, especially on a biscuit, but I have a feeling that's not the kind of sausage the menu's referring to. "You should try it."

"Uhhh…no, thanks. I'll stick with the fish and chips."

"I think I want the clam chowder." Mary's eyes never stray from the menu when Sean comes back with our drinks. He takes our orders and promises to be back as quickly as he can with our food.

"He likes you," I tease when she finally looks up. "He kept staring at you."

Her face turns pink again. "No, he was just doing his job."

"Emma's right. That boy was smitten."

Ever since Mary spent a year locked away with a Fallen Angel, she's never been the same. She hasn't ever told me what happened to her while she was there, but as timid as she is around men now, I have my suspicions. I don't press her because I know what it's like to be nagged when it comes to bad memories. You either want to talk about them or you don't. Dan tries to get me to open up to him all the time about my own experiences, but some things are best left alone.

Taking pity on her, I distract Lila. "So, *Grandmère*, what can you tell us about these people coming from West Virginia tomorrow? Anything important we need to know?"

Lila's face darkens, not a good sign. "The Blackburnes have a bit of a reputation around these parts."

"Worse than ours?" My arm tingles, and I rub at it absently.

"Is your arm okay?" Lila puts her glass of iced tea down and stares at my arm. "Are you sure Silas got the metal out?"

"Yes, I can assure you he did because I felt every ounce of pain while he did it."

"He didn't put you to sleep?"

"This *is* Silas we're talking about."

"For a demon who professes to love you, he does enjoy your pain."

I shrug. As Lila pointed out, he *is* a

demon. Pain is his thing. "Back to the Blackburnes. Are they worse than the Cranes?"

"We never murdered our own children."

"What?" I almost spew my Coke out of my mouth. They killed their kids?

Lila nods. "There are three main magical Families of Power here in the States—the Winters clan, the Petrovichs, and the Blackburnes. Of the three, the Blackburnes are the most powerful. Their family culled the children who showed no signs of magic so only the purest of blood shone through. There's a bounty on Jason and Alexandria Blackburne's heads, a kill on sight order. The magical community fears them. Given what I've been told of Alexandria's power, they have every right to be afraid."

"Okay, wait. Tell me about these Families of Power. Do they have gifts like we do or…"

Lila laughs. "Poppet, we have gifts, yes, but we are not born with magic in our veins, and we are not witches. Our gifts were obtained through outside means, deals done through the centuries. The families I speak of are witches, real witches who use the magic in the air and in their own blood."

I really need to do some reading before they get here so I can understand their abilities better.

"So, we should be on our guard?" Mary asks, just as confused as I am.

"Sabien Blackburne and his sister, Alesha, are nothing like their father or grandparents. They seem to be decent people who try to help where they can despite the bounty on the children's heads. But...stay on your guard. Despite the way things look, there may be secrets hidden beneath the surface."

Just freaking great. One more thing to worry about.

January 3, 2021, Albany, New York.

August 6, 2035, Lewisburg, West Virginia.

May 3, 2020, New Orleans, Louisiana.

What the...? I turn my head, and every single person I look at, I see a date and a place.

Every single person.

"Emma, honey, what's wrong?"

I shake my head, refusing to look at Lila or Mary. I think I know what this is, and I don't want to see.

"I have to go to the bathroom."

Ducking my head, I get up and move as quickly as I can to the back of the restaurant and into the bathroom, where I lock the door. The mirror beckons, but I refuse to look.

I scream one word.

"Kane!"

There's no stall to duck into and hide from the mirror while I wait for Kane. This is not good. I know what those are. Kane explained it during one of our first lessons together.

Death dates.

I'm seeing the date and place of all those people's deaths. He specifically said I had to be a full-blown reaper to see those, and I'm *not* a full-blown reaper. I'm somewhere in between.

Minutes go by, and I slump to the floor, leaning my back against the wall by the sink. Freaking out isn't quite the expression. I'm well past that stage.

What's taking him so long?

There's a knock on the door, followed by Mary's voice. "Em, you okay?"

"I'm fine."

"You've been in there a long time. There are people here who need to use the bathroom."

"Okay, I'm not fine. I've been throwing up violently. They do not want to come in here right now."

"Em…"

"Please, Mary, I just need a few minutes."

I can't make out what she's saying to the people outside, but I hope she gets them to leave.

"Okay, everyone's gone. Now, tell me what's wrong."

"I can't tell you. I need Kane, and he's not coming."

"Kane?" She's quiet for a minute. "Is this a reaping thing?"

"Yes, Mary. I just need everyone to leave me alone until I can talk to Kane. Please."

"Okay, I'll stand here and make sure no one comes in."

"Thank you," I whisper.

Pulling my knees up, I wrap my arms around them and lay my head on my knees. Where is my freaking reaper tutor?

I can't walk around seeing when all my friends and family will die. How could I keep my mouth shut or not try to stop it? The people upstairs already hate me because I saved Dan long enough for him to choose to stay. What would they do if I stopped the natural deaths of my family?

There's a soft swish in the air, and I look up to see an elderly woman standing a few feet away. She's about sixty or sixty-five, her pixie cut hair styled nicely. She has on a sweater and jeans. Grandmotherly. That's how I would describe her.

"Hello, Emma. I'm Elsie, your new trainer."

What? "Where's Kane?"

"He's been reassigned to other duties."

Reassigned? "I want Kane."

"You have me. Now, what's wrong?"

"What aren't you telling me?" She knows something. I can tell by how she's refusing to look me in the eyes.

"I'm not allowed to discuss your old

tutor. I'm here to help you. Or did you just call him to chat?"

"Do I look like I just called him here to chat?" A drop of sweat rolls down my forehead.

"You do seem distressed." She smiles kindly. "And I'm here to help you."

"No. I don't trust you. Too many of your kind have tried to kill me. I want Kane."

Her eyes harden. "He is…unavailable."

"*Why* is he unavailable?"

Her lips thin. "It's not up for discussion."

"Where. Is. Kane?" I put every ounce of power I have into those three little words, hoping my Voice works on a reaper.

"He's being punished."

"Punished?" I spring up from where I'm sitting. "Punished for what?"

"For ignoring his duties as a reaper to help you play investigator. That is not his job. He was supposed to guide you as a reaper, and that is all."

"You're punishing him for helping me?" Incredulity colors my words.

"That's stupid!"

"No, Emma, it's not. As reapers, we keep the balance between life and death. He ignored his duties, and there were consequences for that, consequences that caused more deaths than necessary. While you and Daniel might have ignored those deaths when he chose to stay, we cannot. As reapers, we must not."

"What, did someone die and he was a minute late or something?"

"No, he was several minutes too late, and those souls were eaten by shades and wraiths."

"There was a shade in my hospital room a while back."

"They're escaping The Between, and we've had no luck in understanding how they're getting out."

"That's not good."

"No, it's not." Worry flashes through her brown eyes, but then they clear. "Now, what can I help with you?"

"When is Kane coming back?"

"He's not. As I said, *I* am your new tutor."

"I don't want you."

"Unfortunately, that's not your decision to make. I'm all you have. If there isn't a problem, I have other things to deal with."

I have a feeling telling this woman I'm seeing death dates would be a mistake. My gut is knotted so tight, it's painful. She's not here to help me. She's here to spy for the people upstairs.

"Go deal with your other things."

She frowns but vanishes.

I can't go back out there like this. I can't.

What am I going to do?

"Rose?"

I almost scream when I hear Rhea whisper my name. She's standing where Elsie was just moments before. Her blonde hair is swept up in some kind of intricate ponytail braid thing, and she's wearing her patented sundress. It's purple today with little white daisies all over it. She's beautiful.

And, thank God, there's no death date flashing over her like a neon sign.

"Don't sneak up on me like that."

"I'm sorry. I was waiting until the reaper left to show myself."

"What are you doing here?"

"I heard you call out for your friend, several times, and became concerned. When I showed up and felt your panic, I decided to wait and make sure you were safe with this new reaper."

"I'm not safe with any of them but Kane, and they've taken him away from me. They said he's being punished for helping me. I think they're hurting him."

"But his job is to help you."

I shake my head. "No, he's been helping me outside of my reaping training. He'll come and help search when it's dangerous for me to do it."

"Rose, that is not his job. Keeping him from attending his deaths, that can throw everything out of balance. Life and death have to be attended to promptly…"

"I get it, okay?" I don't need her to lecture me. "I get he's in trouble because of me." Thinking of him in pain causes me a physical pain. "He's my friend."

Her face softens. "You're worried about him."

"I don't know what they're doing to him. He's been helping me for months, protecting me too."

"Protecting you?"

"His bosses want me dead. They've tried to take me out twice now."

"What?" Her voice is whisper soft, and I look up, startled at the anger in it. "Explain."

Crap. She knew they didn't like me, but I never told her they tried to kill me. I need to watch what I say around a goddess. I'm not sure how much juice she actually has, because she did tell me her strength comes from her followers. As far as I know, no one on Earth worships her, but that doesn't mean in other worlds, other realties, she's not some beloved idol.

"It was nothing. I took care of it."

Her golden eyes turn hard. "Explain, Emma Rose."

She never uses my full name. She's pissed. Not sure having a pissed-off goddess in such a small room is a good thing.

"When Dan got shot in Charlotte, he

was dying. I guess all the fear and the need to save him unlocked the gifts you gave me, and I healed him. They didn't want that and came to stop me. Maybe even to smite me, I'm not sure. Remember I told you I thought they might have been thinking about it?"

"You never said they tried anything."

"They didn't get the chance. I did what I always do. I hit first, and whatever I did, it blew them so far away, none of them have come near me again. Instead, they took Kane away from me."

"You said twice." Her eyes have gone even colder, and I shiver looking into them. "What else?"

"Kane came and got me to help him clear a house. Two other reapers were there. They had orders to kill me. One of them stabbed me with a blessed blade. They knew about my demonic half and what that blade would do to me."

She lets out a hiss, and I push away from her, sensing the rage boiling just under her skin.

"Ezekiel had the cure, I assume?"

I shook my head. "No. Nathaniel did.

He came here as fast as he could. He saved my life."

"Georgina's son?"

"He doesn't think of her as his mother any more than I do."

"He's not a good person."

"Neither's Zeke, but that doesn't mean he doesn't love me."

"Your father is a complicated man." Something like hurt flashes through her eyes.

"Why are you so mad at him?"

"I'm not."

"You're a worse liar than Mary."

"This friend, Kane, what did you mean, he protected you?"

Okay, she doesn't want to talk about Zeke. "He warned me they were out to get me, and he's kept most of my abilities secret from them. If they knew how much had reawakened, they'd want me dead as much as they did right before I killed Deleriel."

"He kept you safe by keeping your secrets from those he is supposed to be loyal to?"

"He tried, but I think they figured out

he's been lying, and now they've taken him. I have to find him."

"Why did you need him earlier? You sounded upset."

Even though I want nothing to do with Rhea because she abandoned me to a psychotic mother, at least she's not trying to murder me now. And I need help.

"I'm seeing death dates."

"That's not possible. Only full reapers have that ability."

"And hence why I panicked and started screaming for Kane."

"You didn't trust the reaper who was here?"

"Would you?"

"No." She glides over to where I'm sitting and sinks down on her knees. "This is a natural ability, something that is meant to help reapers, and so I cannot take it away. I can't even mute it. Reapers were designed so the gods couldn't manipulate them."

"Manipulate them?"

"They have the power of life and death in their hands. Reapers can extend life, or they can take it. Gods are forbidden to take a life needlessly. There was a time in our history when humans and other creatures were our playthings. We caused them pain for no reason until laws were put into place to prevent that by our elders. For many, that was harsh, and so they created reapers. Reapers became our tools to continue our games until our elders discovered what we were up to. They killed many of my kin for disobeying them, and they put a protection spell over all reapers. The gods couldn't touch them. To do so meant our own death. Instantly."

"Harsh."

"So, as you can see, I can't do anything about your reaping abilities. I wish I could."

"After Deleriel, when I said not to bind my reaping abilities, you couldn't then, either?"

"No. When you asked to leave them in place, I was relieved. I didn't want to deny you anything."

Well, I guess even a goddess has her limits.

"I just don't want to look at my family

and see when and where they're going to die. Can you at least prevent that?"

"I can't manipulate you, but I *can* them. I can hide that information from you."

"How?"

"I'll remove them from the Wheel of Fate."

"What? That…they told me doing that to Dan made him and me abominations. Won't they try to hurt them if you do that?"

"They could try, and the way I'm feeling at this moment, it wouldn't bode well for them."

"You won't kill them…will you?"

"No. As much as I want to, I can't. It's forbidden."

Relief sweeps through me until a single thought ruins it all. "What happens if I kill one, maybe accidentally?"

"I do not know, so try not to kill them until I find out."

"Back to this Wheel of Fate thing…"

"You family and your friends will be safe. I'll put my personal protection upon them."

"But if you can't do anything to the reapers, what's to stop them from doing it anyway?"

"I said I couldn't kill them, not that I can't hurt them." The joy shining in her eyes warms my heart. Anything to cause them pain gives me reason to be happy.

"Cutting them off from the Wheel, will it hide their death dates from all the reapers?"

Rhea nods.

"Then do it. If you can guarantee their safety, do it."

"I wish I could mute it for you…"

"No, it's fine. Thank you, Rhea." That sounds genuine, even to me. Dan will be proud.

"You are very welcome, my Rose."

She looks like she wants to hug me, but we're not there yet. I've been thinking a lot about Rhea. Dan and I have had several conversations about her, and he thinks it would be good for me to forgive her and maybe try to be friends, at least. She may never be my mother, but maybe friends.

On impulse, I get up and hug her.

And that connection I felt with Zeke the first time I hugged him? It's right here with Rhea. She feels safe and warm. I can feel how much she loves me. It feels right.

Which scares the crap out of me.

I disentangle myself from her and take several steps back. There are tears in her eyes, and guilt overwhelms me. She's done so much for me. She saved me after Deleriel. Even my mama said to give her a chance.

Part of me wants to. Part of me needs to, but that five-year-old little girl is still very much a part of me, too. She remembers what it's like to love a mother who ended up hurting her so badly she never really got over it. I'm not sure I'll ever get past that. My therapist thinks I can if I try, but the fear of being hurt again is too great.

Rhea smiles, really smiles, and her entire being shimmers with light. That's how happy that one little hug made her.

"Dan and I are getting married."

Her eyes widen.

"You can come to the wedding if you

want to."

The words rush out so fast, I'm not sure she understood them when she just stands there staring at me, her expression unreadable.

"You don't have to if you don't want to…"

"No, I want to." She takes a deep breath and smiles. "I would love to come to your wedding. Thank you, Rose."

I nod. This is me trying to forgive her. Trying to honor my mother's wish and forgive Rhea. It's a small step, but Dan will be proud of me.

"I'll go now and take care of your family. Give me a moment, and then you can rejoin your friend outside."

"My sister," I clarify. "Mary is my sister."

"Your sister."

When she leaves, I sink to my knees and bow my head, suddenly exhausted. All I want to do is go home and hide from my new reality. Knowing when and where a person will die is going to take some time to get used to and even longer to learn to ignore it.

The headache that begins to pound behind my eyes is just the icing on the cake.

Now I have to wait and try to calm down enough not to scare Mary and Lila. But how do I do that when I'm scared myself?

"Mattie!"

"In the bedroom."

I hear him enter the room, but I don't look. I'm buried under the covers, eyes closed tight. Rhea kept her promise and hid the death information for Mary and Lila and supposedly the rest of my family and friends, which basically means the Willows and Ethan. I haven't made many friends, keeping to my family and the few hunters who trust me.

"Whatcha doing under there?"

"Hiding."

"From Lila?"

The amusement in his voice filters through the blankets, and I smile despite how freaked out I am. He knows I went dress shopping with Lila and how much I'd dreaded it.

"She's talking about taking you tux shopping next weekend."

"Say what?" His amusement turns to alarm in two seconds flat. See, I'm not the only one who's scared of my grandmother. Secretly, I'm convinced Zeke is terrified of his own mother, too.

"She's serious."

"God help me."

He pulls the covers back, and I turn over so I can't see him accidentally. I'm afraid Rhea hasn't gotten to him yet. I would never be able to unsee that date.

"What's wrong, Squirt?" Concern replaces everything else, and he sits down on the bed.

"I…" Clearing my throat, I force the words out. "I'm seeing the place and time of people's deaths. It's stamped on them like some buy-one-get-one-free sign, and I can't make it go away."

"Mattie."

The wealth of empathy in that one word tells me he understands.

"I'm so sorry, baby. Maybe Kane can help."

"No, he can't. The reapers found out he was helping me on non-reaper stuff, and they took him away. Elsie, my new trainer, said he's being punished."

"Punished?"

"The way she said it made me think they're hurting him, Dan. It's all my fault. I should never have called him to help me search when it was easier for an invisible person to go through a house. He kept me safe, and now he's paying for it."

The bed moves, and Dan slides in behind me, pulling me into the curve of his body. "It's not your fault, baby. Kane is a grown man and made his own choices. Don't blame yourself for this."

"How can I not?" I whisper. I've been lying here for over an hour thinking about all the ways they might be "punishing" him, and none of them were good. After everything I've lived through, I have an excellent imagination when it comes to pain, torture, and all the psychological horror that goes along with it.

Dan kisses the top of my head. "What can I do?"

"I don't know, but I'm going to rescue him."

"Mattie…"

"Don't try to talk me out of it. He's helped me more times than I can count, and now he's the one who needs help. I won't leave him there for them to do God only knows what. I won't. He's family."

"For a girl who was afraid of the word 'family' when I first met you, you've come a long way and gathered quite a large family around you."

"That's because of you." My voice softens and loses some of the panic. "I'd still be that closed-off nightmare if I hadn't met you."

He tries to turn me to face him, and I refuse.

"No. What if Rhea hasn't gotten to you yet, and I see the day you die?"

"What are you talking about, sweetheart? When did you see Rhea?"

I explain to him what she told me about reapers and how she promised to hide my family's death dates from me.

"Baby, you can turn around."

"No. I'm afraid, Dan. What if your date is still there and I see it? I can't handle that."

"My thread has already been cut from the Wheel of Fate, sweetheart. Don't you remember?"

I heave out a sigh. No, I'd been too freaked out to remember that. When he died, Silas essentially cut his string, and it hid him from all reapers. Kane only found him again because of me. Relief sweeps through me, and I open my eyes and turn my head slowly so I can look up at him, still half afraid he's wrong.

And all I see are those warm, brown puppy dog eyes of his, so full of love my heart aches for fear of ever losing it.

"See, baby? I'm all good."

I lunge up and hug him so fiercely it rivals his bear hugs. Dan gives the tightest hugs of anyone I know.

"Easy, there, Hulkster. I can barely breathe," he whispers against my ear. It's only then I notice the slight flinch when my arm shifts against him.

"What's wrong?" I demand, instantly worried.

"Nothing."

"Don't you dare lie to me, Daniel Aaron Richards. I will call Lila and tattle on you."

"You wouldn't dare."

"Try me."

He glares, but there's no heat in it. "It's really nothing. I just got into a little scuffle with a suspect today."

"Scuffle?" Before he can stop me, I lift his shirt and see one entire half of his body is bruised, and his ribs are wrapped. "Oh, my God, Dan. Are you okay?"

"It looks worse than it is."

"Liar. I've had cracked and broken ribs before. I know how bad they hurt."

"When have you had busted ribs?"

"When I was in foster care. I tangled with one of my older foster brothers who decided I was his new bed toy because I was little."

"My God…"

"I don't think about that stuff anymore, Dan. You gave me good memories to replace all those old ones. Don't you start obsessing on something you had no control over."

"It's not that easy, Mattie."

"I know," I say softly. "It's not that easy for me to forget, either, but now is not the time for that conversation."

"What happened? And don't give me that bull about you not being able to talk about an open case. You're not on regular detective duty. You're on supernatural detective duty, and that means you're in *my* realm of expertise. Spill."

"We were tracking someone suspected of being a werewolf."

"Suspected?"

"It's not that easy to know until they change on a full moon. Weres aren't shifters. They can't control when and where they turn. Most aren't even aware of being something more than human. This one we were able to track only because on every bit of surveillance video we were able to find, he was the common element. Delaney and I went to his house to ask some questions. He has a record, and when two cops showed up on his doorstep, he ran. We chased him, and

I was the one to catch him first. I think the insane super strength he exhibited is a clear indication he's the were."

"But you won't know until the full moon?"

Dan shrugs. "The sarge has a resident witch he keeps on call. She's supposed to come in tomorrow and do some kind of spell to tell us if he's a were."

"Does the jail have a special holding cell for supernatural criminals?"

"We do. It's in a different building altogether. It's where my new office is going to be. Thanks to some funding that came in through a huge donation, the Spook Squad of the NOPD will be housed in a swanky historical building. The cells have already been built in the basement, and the upstairs is being turned into headquarters, complete with a few bedrooms that are being turned into dorms for when we have to pull an all-nighter."

Zeke did that. He didn't want Dan to know, and I agreed. My soon-to-be husband would not appreciate it. He'd see it as Zeke interfering when that's the farthest thing from the truth. He's only trying to help.

Now, if Dan ever asked me outright, I'd tell him the truth. I won't lie to him, but if he never asks, then that's that. No muss, no fuss.

His arms snake around me, and try as I might, he still manages to tug me down on top of him.

"Your ribs!"

"Having you here is worth it." He leans up and kisses me. "You're the only medicine I'll ever need."

"Dan…"

"Mattie…" His lips trail down my neck, and my eyes close. He knows exactly how he affects me.

"Not fair."

"Who ever said I was fair?"

"Enough," I say when he hisses in pain. I disentangle myself and sit Indian style beside him. "I'm not going to be responsible for you hurting more than you are."

"Baby…"

"Don't you 'baby' me." I wag my finger at him. "I know what you're up to.

You're trying to distract me from everything I'm hiding from."

He smiles, his white teeth flashing in the semidarkness of the room. That smile of his is more charming than it should be.

"Is it working?"

"Yes." My voice is as grumpy as I feel.

"Then all the pain was worth it."

I gasp. "You are in pain! I knew it."

He laughs but stops abruptly, wincing.

"Don't laugh. It makes it hurt worse. Go take a shower, and I'll see if there's something I can fix for dinner. If not, I'll call Mary and have her grab something on the way over."

"Uh, Squirt, why don't we just order in?"

"No. You deserve a home-cooked meal."

He looks so pained, I almost laugh. He doesn't want to say he hates my cooking, but I hate my cooking, too. I burn water.

"Mary promised to cook."

Relief washes through his eyes. "Want to join me in the shower?"

"Nope. You're hurt, and like I said, I'm not going to be responsible for you hurting worse tomorrow. Deal with it, Officer Dan."

He laughs but gets up and grabs a pair of sweats and a t-shirt.

"Something else I meant to tell you before you distracted me."

"Really? You're the one who kissed me." I try to look pious but fail miserably.

"I found some information for Cass."

That dries up all my laughter. Cass asked me and Dan to help him look into his background. We recently found out he's not quite human, but his uncle refused to tell him anything resembling the truth. So he turned to us.

"And?"

"And his mother didn't exist until a year after he was born. At least not on paper."

"What does that mean?"

"Usually the witness protection program, but I don't think that's the case here unless the supernatural world has the same type of protection program in place the feds do."

"Can you ask James?"

"Yeah, I planned on calling him later to check."

"I hear a 'but' in there."

"But I don't think they do. We know his mother was the supernatural creature because all the Willows are human."

"Maybe not. His uncle told him no matter what, he was a Willow. Maybe his mother wasn't the supernatural. Maybe it was his biological father. Maybe that's who she was hiding from and that's why all her information is fake."

"That's a lot of maybes."

I shrug. "Yeah, but we'll figure it out."

"We will. I'm gonna go take a shower, so please don't burn the place down until Mary gets here."

"I won't even turn the stove on."

I'm pretty sure he mutters, "Thank God," under his breath, but I let it slide. He's hurt, and he does deserve a home-cooked meal. Mary is the better cook. Mrs. B started giving us both cooking lessons, but I'm still not very good. I set the kitchen on fire just yesterday at Zeke's.

It was embarrassing.

Zeke even suggested maybe I should hire a cook when Dan and I get married. I started to brush it off, but if I don't get better at this whole cooking thing, I'd rather hold my tongue than starve my husband.

Husband.

Last year, I would have freaked out over that word.

But all it does now is give me a thrill of anticipation. It means safety, security, and someone who loves me despite myself. It means home.

The kitchen proves Dan and I haven't been shopping this week. I just got out of the hospital a few days ago, and with the threat from Kristof hanging over me, I haven't really been anywhere to do any shopping. I'm either here or at Zeke's.

Kristoff warned me to play by the rules, but so far, the dead man's blood I keep in my system has kept him out of my head. I'm afraid he's going to get irritated sooner rather than later and take it out on someone I love. Which is why Mary has a bodyguard in the form of my brother Nathaniel. She doesn't go anywhere without him. I trust him to keep her safe more than anyone else. He's a Dubois and therefore has no qualms about using black magic or demon curses to get what he wants. Or, in this case, the lengths to which he'll go to keep Mary safe.

The fridge holds most of what we need for chicken alfredo. Fresh broccoli is all we're missing, so I text her to stop at the store to pick up some. Personally, I refuse to eat broccoli, but Dan and Mary like it, so I relented. The things I do for family.

I flop down on the couch and pick up my Kindle to wait until either Dan gets out of the shower or Mary shows up with my brother in tow.

"I swear by all that's holy, I will beat you, Nathaniel!"

Dan and I look from the door to each other and back again.

"I only…"

"Move before I stomp your foot."

What is going on? Dan mouths, not wanting to speak and interrupt Mary and Nathaniel's hallway argument.

"Woman, I was only…"

"Oh, for Pete's sake…"

There are several loud thumps, a grunt, and then the key slides into the lock. Mary waltzes in, carrying a paper grocery bag. Nathaniel follows, scowling and limping.

"Do I want to ask?" Dan leans back against the couch and throws an arm around me.

"He's an idiot." Mary puts the bag down on the kitchen island.

Nathaniel's eyes narrow, but he sighs. "Where do you want the package?"

"Package?" It's only then I notice he's carrying a rather large cardboard box.

"It was at the front desk. They were about to call you, but I said I'd bring it up."

"Let me see." I disentangle myself from Dan and motion for Nathaniel to put the box on the coffee table in front of us. It's bulky, but not heavy. It also doesn't say who it's from. "Mary, can you grab a knife from the kitchen so I can open it?"

"No need." Dan pulls out a pocketknife and opens it for me. "There you go, Squirt."

An odor tickles my nose as soon as I push aside the flaps. A foul odor.

Dan pushes me back before I can say anything and shoves the entire table away from us. "Move!"

It all happens so fast, yet it's like one

of those slow-motion scenes in a movie. One second, we are all happily chatting, and the next an explosion rips through the room, and we're airborne, flying backward into the wall.

An eerie silence descends into the chaos as glass and plaster rain down upon us. I blink, trying to clear my blurry vision. My ears are ringing, and dust and more plaster falls in pieces around us. I feel light as a feather, but I can't move.

And then the ringing lessens, allowing in other sounds.

Screaming.

Shouting.

But, oddly, what's the loudest to me is the beeping of the smoke detector. I don't know why I can hear it so clearly when everything else is muted.

Hands shake me, and I stare up into worried brown eyes. He's saying something, but I don't understand. I can see his lips moving, but it's like I'm underwater, and the only real thing I can hear is the danged smoke detector.

Blood drips down his face and splatters my cheek. He's bleeding. I reach up, intending to swipe the blood away, but he grasps my hand and pulls me to my feet. I sway, but he catches me before I can fall.

I do my best to focus on the sound of his voice, but again, it's barely audible.

"You're bleeding," he frets and pulls his shirt off to hold to my head. The bruises on his body remind me he'd been injured earlier. He has to be in so much pain.

"I…I can barely hear you."

He frowns and shakes his head.

"I know, baby. I can't hear, either. It's the blast. Our hearing will come back. Give it a few minutes."

He speaks slowly, and I am able to understand most of what he says by reading his lips. I guess it makes sense. The big bang did some damage to our eardrums. Dan and I were the closest to the box.

I take a step toward him, and my knees buckle. He catches me again and lowers me back to the ground.

"Sit here. I need to check on Nathaniel and Mary."

My eyes widen. Oh, my God. I'd

forgotten all about them. Dan scrambles over the busted furniture into the kitchen. His back is turned, and I want to shout, but he won't hear me. It's not until I see Nathaniel and Mary emerge from behind the island that my heart rate calms the tiniest bit.

Thank God.

Nathaniel shakes his head, and Mary stumbles when she steps out. My brother catches her, and for once, Mary doesn't try to shake him off. Goes to show how out of sorts she is. Instead, she leans heavily on him as they make their way to me. She sits down next to me, and I don't hesitate. I hug her. I know she's freaking out the same way I am. After everything we've been through, any kind of trauma upsets us and brings those old memories back. I know I'm fighting to keep them at bay, so she probably is, too.

"Emma?" Nathaniel squats in front of me. "Are you okay?"

I nod. I don't think anything's broken. I'm just sore, and my shoulder hurts where it slammed into the ground.

Nathaniel kisses my forehead and

stands, turning to talk to Dan.

Mary's shaking, and I pull her closer. I'm shaking, too, and need the comfort as much as she does.

It's not long before police and paramedics swarm the apartment. Dan keeps looking toward me as he speaks with police. I let the paramedics clean up my cuts but refuse to go the hospital. I'm not that hurt. Mary does the same. We're both banged up with cuts and bruises, but otherwise we're okay.

Had Dan not shoved the table away, I might not be so okay. Him, either. We might have been really hurt. Heck, I might have lost a hand if I'd reached in without looking. It could have been so much worse.

The ringing in my ears is almost gone by the time the detective comes over to me. I'd guess she's somewhere in her late thirties, early forties, maybe. Her hair is dark brown, and she's got it pulled back in a very severe bun. She's dressed in jeans and a nice blouse. Not at all what I'm used to. Most detectives, men and women, wear suits or dress clothes. Jeans is not their average attire. I applaud her for choosing comfort over formality.

March 28, 2020. New Orleans.

I try to will away the knowledge of her death, but it's right there flashing above her head. I risk a look around then stare down at the floor. Everyone's death date is still there. How am I going to get used to this?

"Miss Crane, I'm Detective Ashlyn Farr. I work with Dan."

My gaze swings to him. Why is his spook squad here instead of the regular police?

"You're wondering what I'm doing here, huh?" She smiles, and I frown. "Your face is pretty much an open book right now."

Well, fudgepops.

"It was the smell that was coming out of the box that has me here. Dan texted us, and we took over the case."

The smell. I nod slowly, trying to remember what it smelled like. "It was foul."

"It was dead man's blood."

"What?" I should have known that.

I've had to drink enough of the crap the last few days. "It didn't smell like that, though."

"That's because it was fresh, not aged. It smells worse when you collect it from a new corpse."

"That makes no sense. If it's old, it should curdle or something."

"You'd think, wouldn't you?" Her green eyes are serious, so I know she isn't attempting a joke. "It's odd, but that's just the way it is."

Huh.

"Are you up for answering a few questions?"

"Yeah…I mean yes."

"Do you remember anything about the box? A return address, weird markings or the like?"

"No. There wasn't a return address. It just had my name on it, which I guess is weird itself."

"Why's that?"

"Because my name's not on the lease. No one would know to send me anything here."

"Are you here a lot?"

"Yeah, but I don't live here."

"But people know you and Dan are engaged and that he lives here, so it would stand to reason you spend a lot of time here, yes?"

"I guess."

"So someone may know that."

"I guess."

Jeez, did I have an answer besides "I guess?" I must really be rattled.

"Is there anyone who might want to hurt you?"

I'm not sure what I should tell her. I don't know her, and therefore I don't trust her.

"My dad has made a lot of enemies who might think they can hurt him by coming after me."

"We'll definitely be looking into that, but is there anyone who has a grudge against you specifically?"

Most cops don't ask a question they don't already know the answer to, something I learned from Detective Grady back in North Carolina. Sometimes they don't, but more often than not, they do. Still, she might be fishing for information.

Dan comes over, sensing my unease from across the room. I think even without the soul bond, he'd still feel me. It's a truth I know in my heart. I knew it from the very beginning. It's what drove him to find me when I went missing all those years ago. It's what drove him to follow up on a crazy story appearing on his computer screen when he couldn't explain it. He loves me, and that love will always drive him in ways a lot of people can't understand because they've never felt it. But we have it, and I thank God every day. For Dan.

"Why don't we take this to the bedroom?"

Detective Farr agrees, and Dan helps me to stand. I look for Mary, but she's being bandaged up. Nathaniel is right beside her. He nods toward me to say he's got her, and I let Dan lead me into the bedroom. The bed is a welcome relief. Sitting on the hard floor for long periods is not fun. I have no idea how little kids do it.

Dan closes the door behind us and

comes to sit by me. "You can trust her, Squirt."

Just because he trusts her doesn't mean I do.

"She has issues with police," he says when I stay silent.

"I can tell." Detective Farr tries to smile, but it doesn't quite reach her eyes.

"What do you want to know?" Dan pulls me closer, and I lean into his side, seeking warmth. He's not that much warmer than I am anymore, but I'll take what I can get.

"I was asking Miss Crane if there was anyone who specifically had a grudge against her."

"Kristoff."

My fingers dig into his side. He didn't need to go and tell her that. It was something we were handling privately with the hunting community. No need to involve the police.

"Who is Kristoff?"

"An insane vampire who thinks Mattie is his new plaything." Dan looks down at me, his expression softening. "You need to tell her, Mattie."

"We don't know this is him," I argue grumpily. "It's not even dark yet."

"I'm not sure if you are aware of what is commonly referred to as a human servant...the eyes and ears of a vampire while they sleep. This person goes where a vampire can't, even at night. They are bound to the vampire through blood and are exceptionally loyal."

"I am aware."

"Then you realize this bomb may have been Kristoff's work through his human servant."

"It's possible." I don't think so, but it's possible.

"Or it could be people he paid." Dan rubs my back soothingly. "One thing I've come to learn about the supernatural world is they are just as capable of dealing with humans as we are them."

"That's true enough," Detective Farr agrees. "Still, I'd like to look into the Kristoff angle. Tell me about him."

"He's old, hundreds of years old." I sit up and away from Dan, wrapping my arm around myself. "He's a serial killer."

Detective Farr's eyes sharpen. "How

do you know?"

"Do you know what a hunter is?"

Her lip curls. See, this is why I have trust issues with the police.

"Vigilantes."

"No, they're not. They're the people who have been trained to hunt down the supernatural creatures the rest of the world doesn't know about. They are far better equipped than the police to deal with the threat."

Dan holds up his hand to stop whatever the detective is about to say. "Just agree to disagree."

"Anyway. I was asked to help a friend look for a missing hunter. We ended up tracking her down to a house deep in the bayou. We found her there barely alive but managed to get out before Kristoff woke up. He came to the hospital to see me."

My arm aches with the memory of him snapping the bone, and I shrink away from it. He scared me in ways no one else had, not even the blood demon I vanquished at Christmas.

"And?" Detective Farr prompts when I

don't say anything else.

"And he informed me I was his new plaything since I'd stolen his last one. He said I had to follow the rules or the people I loved would get hurt."

"Rules?"

I nod, remembering how crazy he looked when he told me that. "If I didn't do as he said, he'd go after the people I loved. It was his only rule."

Detective Farr makes notes in a little pad. "Have you followed his rules?"

"No. I've been drinking dead man's blood daily. It's why I was so surprised I didn't recognize it."

"I would advise to keep drinking it. If a vampire gets in your head, there's nothing you can do. They have you."

Like I don't know this? There's no other reason I'd willingly drink blood.

"This might not be about me, though."

That got both their attention.

"It could be Dan. He is a cop, after all, and I'm sure he's pissed off more than a few people in the supernatural world."

"The package was addressed to you, though." Detective Farr didn't even look up from scribbling with that little nugget of wisdom.

"You were the one who pointed out people know I'm here as much as I'm at home or at school. The best way to hurt Dan is to hurt me."

The woman studies me for a long moment before shifting her gaze to Dan. "You're right about her."

He grins. "Told you."

"What are you two talking about?"

"Dan told me that you have the mind of a police officer, and he's right. Your mind works like ours do, continually looking for different angles and shifting the theory of the crime to fit the one that makes the most sense until it's either proven or debunked."

"I am *not* a cop." The very thought gives me hives. Police were not very good to me when I was younger, and it's not something I'll ever forget. Dan gets a pass because…well…he's Dan.

"We could always use more good officers who know about the supernatural."

The stare I level her with is one I've

used to fell far greater people than her, and she's no different. She takes a step back. I might be short and petite, but I can intimidate with the best of them.

"Squirt…" Dan sighs. He knows me, so he should have known how I'd react. Police and I do not mix. As I said before, Dan is the exception to the rule.

"Is there anything else you can think of, Miss Crane?" Detective Farr shifts back into police mode, and she doesn't look quite as friendly as before. "Do you remember seeing anyone strange or suspicious following you today? Anyone downstairs you didn't recognize when you came up?"

"No, but I wasn't looking, either. I was out wedding dress shopping with my grandmother and my sister."

"Sister? I wasn't aware Ezekiel Crane had another daughter."

"He doesn't, but she's my sister, blood or no blood."

She jots down another note, probably to look into the so-called sister.

"And what's your sister's name?"

See? I knew it. "Mary Cross. You

spoke to her earlier. The paramedics are still cleaning up her cuts out front if you need to talk to her again." Another scribble in her notebook. "Are we done? It's getting late, and I need to be indoors before dark."

"For now. Where will you be if we have more follow-up questions?"

"At my father's."

"And Miss Cross will be there as well?"

"Of course."

"Then we're done for now. Dan, can I talk to you for a moment?"

"Sure." He drops a kiss onto my forehead and follows the snooty detective back out into the hallway, closing the door behind him.

I hate snooty people, especially police. Aside from her choice of clothing, I don't think I like her. She fixated on Kristoff, ignoring all the other possibilities. I know Dan won't ignore them, even if they tell him he's not allowed to investigate because he was a victim of the crime.

There's a knock, and then Mary and Nathaniel come in, looking tired. Both their faces are streaked with dirt, and they look a little bedraggled, truth be told. Mary is also leaning into Nathaniel, who looks concerned.

"You okay?" I pat the bed next to me, and she walks slowly over, limping.

"My leg's bothering me. I think I landed on it wrong when Nathaniel pushed me down."

"I keep telling her she needs to go to the ER."

"No, she doesn't." Mary's leg was never the same after her time with Mrs. Olsen. She'll always walk with a limp because of the torture she suffered. Falling must have aggravated it.

"But..."

I shake my head, my eyes warning him to shut up. She has enough to deal with without explaining why she's limping. She squeezes my hand gratefully.

"You're staying at Zeke's with us." I know he has his own place, but after what happened, I'm not trusting that something similar won't happen to him. Sure, I'd told the detective it could be someone besides Kristoff, but it could be him, too. I'm not ruling him out like she's ruled out every other possibility.

"That's not really necessary." My brother's southern drawl is quite charming, but I will not be swayed. I've lost enough people to last me a lifetime.

"Yes, Nathaniel, it *is* necessary. Zeke's is warded against every possible thing you can think of. We were all almost blown up. I need everyone to be somewhere safe, and that includes you."

"I can take care of myself."

"So can I, but look at what happened."

My father doesn't like him, and I'm not sure if Nathaniel doesn't like Zeke or is just wary of him. The two of them don't talk unless forced to. Granted, it was his family who sold my soul to a Fallen Angel for a blood debt they owed, but Nathaniel doesn't seem to want me dead.

Yet.

Which is where my father's unease comes into play. He's worried if Nathaniel ever finds out what I am, he'll want my gifts. The only way to obtain them is to kill me and consume my blood. Icky, but true.

"Emma…"

"Don't 'Emma' me. You're coming, and that's that."

His face softens. "The bomb really shook you, didn't it?"

I nod. "If Dan hadn't been there…"

Mary's fingers tighten around mine. "Don't think about it."

"She's right." Nathaniel sits on my other side. "There's no use in thinking about the what-ifs. It doesn't help and will drive you insane."

"What will drive me insane is wondering if you're safe or not, so don't argue about coming with us to Zeke's. My father won't bite you."

"You sure about that?"

I wasn't, but I didn't tell him that. "Please, Nathaniel?"

"Fine, but only because you survived a bomb."

"Thank you."

Mary leans into me. "Can we go now?"

"The police already talk to you?"

Nathaniel's face darkens. "Yes."

"What's that look for?"

"I don't like police."

Something we have in common, but I think it's deeper than that. "What did the snooty detective say to you?"

"She asked him if he had something to do with the bomb."

Nathaniel shoots Mary a glare, which she only stares him down for. He looks away first. Interesting.

"That's stupid. If you were going to blow me up, you wouldn't be anywhere near me. You could have died, too."

"At least you trust me."

"I do." The answer is immediate and without hesitation, shocking me as much as him. I still have that warning in my bones that says to be cautious, but for once, I can ignore it. He's proven himself time and time again. The true test will be when or if I ever decide to tell him about my true heritage, but for now, I trust him.

Mary sits up and glances at me curiously. She knows all about my misgivings when it comes to my brother. She doesn't trust him as far as she can throw him, so I understand her curiosity as to my answer.

"You do?" she asks, her expression almost somber.

"Yeah, I do."

"Okay, then."

And that's that. She shifts her opinion of my brother because I have. Doesn't mean she necessarily likes him, but she might not be so suspicious of him anymore.

"What just happened there?" Nathaniel asks.

"We decided you're family."

"But I *am* your family. We have the same mother."

Mary smiles. "Our family—me, Mattie, Eric, and Ethan—we're family because we chose to be, not because we're bound by blood. They're our brothers, and we're their sisters. Family you choose is more important than the family you're born into. We chose to make you part of our family, Nathaniel. Just don't screw it up."

He blinks several times, his gaze swinging from me to Mary. He understands how important the moment is, but I think he's speechless. I can see it in his eyes. He wasn't expecting either of us to say that.

Dan opens the door, saving Nathaniel from having to say anything in response to our bombshell. "You guys ready to go?"

"Yeah, let's go get my father's nervous breakdown out of the way. You know he's going to flip out."

Dan shakes his head, his expression weary. "Yeah, best to get that over with before our guests from West Virginia arrive tomorrow."

Snap, I forgot about that. Dan's right, it's better to get Zeke's freak-out moment over and done with before they get here and he scares the crap out of all of them.

The three of us get off the bed and trek through the living room now crawling with police officers. The place is a mess, and the Christmas tree I didn't have the heart to take down is laying scattered in pieces throughout the room. Poor thing.

Now to go find my father before he hears about the bombing and starts blowing up my phone.

God save me.

Saidie

New Orleans, LA

The best thing about a private plane? We don't have to worry about a ton of other passengers disembarking. Which is a good thing because my boyfriend has stopped at the bottom of the steps and has his face upturned toward the sun, a look of wonder taking over his expression.

He hasn't been able to stand in the sunlight for almost eight years without fear of being burned like a crispy critter. Vampires don't explode in the sun like movies and books portray. It's actually a lot worse. Their skin starts to smoke, and then it cooks and blisters into horrible third-degree burns. The pain is unbearable, or so Aleric says.

He gets this haunted, terrified look in his eyes when he talks about it. I know without him having to say anything that Madame tortured him like this. She was never kind to him or his vampire brothers. She was cruel. I plan on making sure every single one of those haunted looks gets replaced by a good memory. He deserves happiness.

Alex's mom, Alesha Blackburne, made him a talisman that allows him to walk in the sun in the form of a toe ring. I was a little put off at first, thinking it would be a ring like Stefan and Damon wore in *The Vampire Diaries*. Even a necklace would do, but a toe ring?

Alesha explained a ring or necklace would be too obvious, especially if Kristoff finds out Aleric is walking around in the bright light of day. The toe ring will be out of sight with no one the wiser.

I'm all for anything that keeps my man

safe from a deranged vampire.

"Dude, you're holding up the line," Conner grouches from behind us.

Aleric turns his head and stares. Conner stares right back, unperturbed. Nothing scares him, and as far as I know, he can't be intimidated, not even by Luka, and Luka intimidates everyone. Including my boyfriend, who is his brother.

"Come on, we need to get to the hotel, anyway. We can go for a walk or something once we're checked in."

He smiles, and my heart does this weird fluttering thing. He's beautiful with his Romani dark looks and those brilliant green eyes of his. He steals my breath away without even trying.

"Wha'ever you want, *bon fille.*"

He takes my hand, and we continue into the airport. Alex catches up a minute later. She has on dark sunglasses. Her eyes bother her in direct sunlight. A side effect of absorbing some of Aleric's vampirism is that her eyes, which were sensitive to sunlight before, have now become downright hostile when dealing with bright lights of any kind. She gets irritated with it.

"Hey, Uncle Sabien says Mr. Crane should have a car waiting for us. We're not going straight to the hotel. We're going to his house first."

"Dat wasn't de plan." Aleric's gaze swings to his brother, who is right behind Alex.

"I no like it, either." Luka shakes his head, his own green eyes cold. The brothers might share the same color eyes, but that's where the similarities end. Luka's eyes are always cold unless he's looking at Alex. Then they remind me of Aleric's, whose are usually at least not giving off the back-off-or-I'll-murder-you vibe. The only things that matter to Luka are Alex and his brother. He couldn't care less about friends or what others think of him. He's scary, and that's saying something coming from the girlfriend of a vampire.

"It's not a big deal." Alex rolls her eyes. "We were invited here by the Cranes to help them with a problem. You're both acting like they mean us harm or something."

"De name Crane is well known in dese parts." Aleric looks around, his eyes assessing. "Most folks roun' here doan get on de bad side of a Crane. Even Madame wouldn't cross dem. Dey are no' good people."

Luka's lips thin, and his eyes grow even colder. He'd looked at me like that once upon a time when he wanted to kill me for being a Necromancer. He hates them, but because I'm tied to his brother now, he's backed off. Not entirely, but enough so I'm not worried he'll stab me to death in my sleep. Progress.

"Can you guys believe how warm it is?" Jason Reed rolls to a stop beside where we're collecting our luggage. "If I'd known it'd be this warm, I would have brought shorts."

"You'd get sick," Bree tells him.

"I'm a shifter. We don't get sick," he counters with a grin. Bree shakes her head. The two of them are cute together. She's not his mate, though. At least according to Alex. I'm gonna trust her on this since I have no idea about how shifters seem to just know their mate when they meet. I hope Bree doesn't get hurt when Jason finally finds his.

I glance back to see Micah, Sabien, and Alesha trailing behind us. Micah looks tired. He's a shifter, too, and linked to Alex in a way I don't understand, but they seem to share the same mind sometimes. They hear each other's thoughts. It's weird, and I'm surprised Luka doesn't want to rip the guy apart, but Micah is the only person he trusts with Alex.

"What's wrong with Micah?"

"He was up late. Bad breakup with his girlfriend," Alex whispers against my ear so softly I can barely hear it, but with so many shifters, their hearing is superb.

"Ouch."

She nods. She mouths, *"He got a little drunk."*

We get our luggage and start walking toward the exit. A man wearing a black suit is holding up a sign with my name on it. This must be the driver.

"Excuse me…"

"Miss Walker, are the rest of your

party here as well?" I expected him to have a southern drawl or a New Orleans accent, but he doesn't. His tone is rather bland.

"Yes." I gesture behind us where the last of our crew is getting their luggage.

"Very good, miss. We have two cars waiting to take everyone to Mr. Crane's plantation."

Two large limos are waiting for us. I didn't expect that. I thought maybe some town cars or something, but not this. I've never been in a limousine before. The inside is as nice as you see on TV, and the seats are like sitting on air. It's amazing. There's a mini fridge and phone as well.

"Feel free to avail yourselves of anything in the refrigerator." The driver holds the door while Alex, Luka, Micah, and Conner get in the car. Everyone else gets in the other limo.

"Wow, this is nice." Conner's gaze travels over everything as he settles in. "Fancy."

"Mom said the Cranes were rich." Alex grips Luka's hand and huddles into him. He makes a soothing noise and kisses her forehead.

"You okay?" I ask.

She nods, a small smile slipping out. "Sometimes I still hear him in my head, and I have to remind myself that this reality is the one I chose to be real. I can hear him calling to me now."

I hate that she still suffers from her grandfather's attack on her. He made her think she was crazy, that this reality was made up, and all she had to do was choose to remain in the real world, the world without magic, the world without *us*.

In that other place, she told me Jason hated her for attacking him when she was out of her mind. The Jason here loves his sister and would move mountains to keep her safe. I wouldn't willingly choose a reality where my brother hated me, either.

"We're here to help you when you need it. Just ask."

She nods again and snuggles into Luka. "Usually Luka is enough, but sometimes his voice is so loud, I need more than Luka. Jason helps me most then."

Him would be her grandfather. When she slipped into her coma a few months back, it was caused by her grandfather, and he built a whole reality where she was still in the mental hospital and everything she'd experienced here was explainable there. She told me it was as real to her as this reality is. In her dream, her grandfather was her doctor. While he might be dead now, he still haunts her dreams. He did such a number on her, that reality still breaks through to this one in her mind. If I had the man in front of me, I'd kill him again. Slowly.

Alex is the sweetest person I've ever met, and she doesn't deserve to go through what she is. She deserves to be happy and nightmare free. Thanks to that old man, I don't know if that'll ever happen.

Micah moves to sit on Alex's other side and presses close against her. She sighs and reaches out to take one of his hands and wraps it around her middle. His chin rests on her shoulder, and she's literally surrounded by Luka and Micah. Luka doesn't bat an eye. She needs them both, and he understands that.

"It's okay, Blue," Micah whispers. "We got you. You're not alone."

"I know."

"Guys, I don't want to alarm you, but I've been having visions since we landed."

We all look at Conner, whose strange purple eyes are so unfocused, it's not even funny.

"There are bad things coming for all of us." He shakes his head. "Dead things."

Conner is a Seer, thanks to his Celtic heritage. He inherited The Sight from his grandmother and has visions. When he's around Alex, they're stronger, so I don't doubt a word he's saying.

"They're coming for me, Conner. As long as you guys stay away from the mansion, you'll be safe."

"Not a chance," Alex rebuts. "We're not letting you go there alone. We'll all go."

Luka looks like he wants to argue, but Micah speaks. "We're stronger together,

Saidie."

I don't want any of them near that place, but I can see arguing is pointless.

Conner gets a bottle of water out of the fridge and takes a long swallow. "He's right. If you go alone, you'll die. That's part of what I saw. If we go together, it'll be dangerous, but I don't think anyone will die."

"Doan t'ink? You doan know?" Aleric growls, his hand tightening around me.

"My visions aren't always clear. I just see danger, dead things swarming, and Saidie dying alone. She's not stepping foot in that place without us."

Well, hell.

"No more arguing," Alex says and snuggles into her boys. "Let's just enjoy the ride and worry once we get all the facts."

She's right. Without knowing everything, there's no point in worrying. I settle into Aleric and rest my head on his chest. His heartbeat is strong. Vampires don't have a heartbeat, but my magic restarted his. It's the most beautiful sound in the world to me.

All we can do now is wait.

The car slows, and I look out the window to see we're passing a gate and driving up a long driveway lined with trees, providing shade for the entire length of the driveway. The house is beautiful, a three-story mansion with large pillars along the front. There are rocking chairs and a small table with chairs on the front porch. I can see gardens to the left and right. It's magnificent. More beautiful even than Madame's bayou mansion.

When we stop, the driver gets out and opens the door for us. We all pile out and stand there, taking in the beauty around us. I'd heard New Orleans had mansions even grander than those in Georgia, but I hadn't believed it until now. This one blows all the others I've seen out of the water.

"Fancy," Jason remarks and shoves his hands in his pockets. "Think we should touch anything?" All the women, including his mother, glare, and he shrugs. "It was a legit question."

With Jason, it probably is. For a guy who's a monster on the football field, he has a habit of breaking things. He probably shouldn't touch anything.

"Come along, children." Sabien walks up the porch steps and knocks firmly on the front door.

An older man dressed in a formal black suit and white shirt answers the door. He smiles warmly. "Mr. Blackburne?"

Sabien nods.

"We've been expecting you. Please, come in, come in."

He moves aside so we can all enter. The front foyer is wide and just as beautiful as the outside. It looks like all the original woodwork has been preserved and well taken care of. The floors are white marble, and the walls have been done in a soft ivory color. Paintings that look as old as the house grace the walls. It's just…wow.

"I'm Jameson, and if you'll all follow me into the parlor, I'll get you refreshments. Mr. Crane is on the phone at the moment. There's a bit of a situation with his daughter."

There are two large couches as well as several other seats in the room. It's more than enough to fit us all. Luka and Aleric do not look comfortable. I wonder if it's that they don't trust Mr. Crane or if it's Aleric's unease about being back in New Orleans and Luka picked up on it. It's hard to tell with those two.

"Jason, put that down!"

Sabien's whisper-shout pulls me out of my thoughts. Jason is holding a very expensive-looking vase. Since Sabien had to hide all his, I can understand him yelling at Jason. He'll break it.

"I was only…" The vase slips, and thankfully, Conner catches it.

"Stop touching things and sit," Sabien hisses at him.

I turn away to hide my smile. Leave it to Jason to give his uncle heart palpitations.

Jameson returns with a pitcher of iced tea and another pitcher of water. "We also have Coca-Cola and orange juice, as Miss Emma loves those drinks. Would any of you like some of that instead?"

My hand goes up at the mention of Coke. I am not a tea drinker. Bree and Conner both ask for the soft drink as well. We need our sugar.

We're all sitting sipping on our cold drinks when a man comes into the room, looking harried. He has long brown hair that's tied back into a ponytail. Sharp blue eyes sweep over us. He reminds me of that actor who plays Ichabod Crane on Fox's *Sleepy Hollow*. It's weird. He could be the guy's twin brother, only this man looks way more dangerous. The vibe he's giving off makes me shrink closer to Aleric. His entire demeanor says, "Don't mess with me or you'll regret it."

"I'm sorry for making you wait. I was on the phone with my future son-in-law." He runs a hand through his hair, the ponytail coming loose with the gesture. His hair lands right at his shoulders. "I'm Ezekiel Crane. Welcome to my home and to New Orleans."

He has a very cultured Creole accent that speaks of old money. It's pleasant to listen to, which is such a stark contrast the dangerous vibe I'm getting from him. He's agitated, and maybe that's why he's so threatening.

"I hope everything is okay," Sabien says and stands. "I'm Sabien Blackburne." He goes around the room, introducing us all.

When he gets to me, Ezekiel's attention lands squarely on me.

"You are the Necromancer?"

I nod, not trusting my voice not to squeak.

"We're grateful you could come on such short notice. The vampire we need to reach has targeted my daughter, so if there's anything you need, anything at all, you only need to ask."

"Targeted your daughter?" Conner asks.

"Yes. Emma Rose is...well, she's

special, and her unique abilities have intrigued him. He's told her that she must play his game, and if she breaks the rules, he'll hurt those she loves."

"What's his name?" I whisper, afraid of what I'm going to hear.

"Kristoff."

A shuddering breath leaves me. Kristoff scares the hell out of me. He was really the only thing Madame threw at me that did scare me. Everything else, I withstood, but I remember the look in his eyes the night I met him. He was a man who enjoyed perverse torture and causing pain.

"You know him?"

"Yes." I barely manage to get the word out. Aleric pulls me into his lap, and I wrap myself around him. He understands my fear. He's been a victim of his brother. Madame used Kristoff to teach Aleric to do as he's told. Even before he was a vampire. Kristoff was his punisher from the moment he was taken by Madame at the age of nine. His heart is beating as rapidly as mine. He's as afraid of him as I am, but he's doing his best to offer me comfort, and I love him for it.

But Kristoff is mine to deal with since I inherited him and all of Madame's other creatures as well as her properties. I don't want any of it, but that doesn't mean I can ignore it.

"You understand how dangerous he is?" Ezekiel presses.

"Trust me, she does." Alex comes to sit beside me. She can't touch me, but her presence helps. "She was held captive by the Necromancer who lived there before and tortured for information."

"Information?" Ezekiel frowns.

"Madame wanted to know where I was."

"Why?"

"That doesn't matter." Alesha's tone leaves no room for questions. "Tell us more about why you called us here. I'm assuming it's more than a vampire running around?"

Ezekiel's eyes narrow, and Alesha's nostrils flare. Something shifts behind her eyes, and the man takes a step back, but Alesha moves forward. Her eyes are dilated, and she's sniffing the air. Alex's breath catches. Something is definitely up.

He recovers quickly. He even steps closer to Alesha, who looks like someone knocked the wind out of her. Alex, Jason, and Micah all look thrown. *What the hell is going on?*

"I'm going to assume the Necromancer wanted to turn your daughter in for the massive bounty?"

"You know about that?"

"There's very little I don't know about. Your children are perfectly safe here since I have a daughter myself I'd do anything to protect. No one would dare touch them here while they're under my protection."

God, he sounds arrogant. Worse than even Luka.

"Then you can tell us what we need to know about the situation." Sabien leans forward in his seat, his eyes sharp.

"The mansion is surrounded by things our hunters can't kill. The creatures cause intense pain when they touch your flesh. We've not been able to breach the island. I'm told the creatures are a form of the dead, hence why we need a Necromancer to put them down."

"It's not that easy," Alesha says. "I know the creatures you're speaking of. They're dead, yes, but it's also a powerful spell that gives them the ability to cause the pain you're describing. It's going to take a witch just as powerful as the Necromancer was to counter the spell so Saidie can put the dead down."

"The Necromancer who lived there before was a witch?" Ezekiel seems surprised.

"I thought you knew everything?" Alesha asks, her tone slightly snide.

"I said there's very little I don't know, not nothing." His blue eyes narrow. "I can find a witch to deal with the spell."

"No need. We can handle that."

"You're saying you're as strong a witch as the Necromancer was?"

"I'm not just stronger, I'm *better*."

"You're quite sure of yourself, aren't you?"

"No more so than you."

I glance at Alex, and her expression is concerned. Alesha and Ezekiel aren't flirting, but they're doing something. Jason doesn't look happy, either. I don't understand any of this.

"Ahem, if we could get back to the subject at hand?" Sabien sounds irritated. "How many of those things are in the water surrounding the island?"

"Dozens." Aleric's expression is haunted. "Dey be dozens in de water. Madame…she wanted to make sure no one cou' hurt her. Dose t'ings, dey be her insurance against attack."

Ezekiel cocks his head. "You sound like you're from the bayou."

"He was a prisoner of hers, too," I say quickly. "He risked his life to get me out."

"You're both very lucky, from what I've been able to discern. We've had three hunters die trying to get past that insurance policy of hers."

"I'll need to go out and see these things for myself to start developing a counter spell." Alesha looks to her children. "I may need your help as well as Bree's. If they're as strong as he says, it could take more than just me. We might need the strength of a coven, and the four of us represent that."

"Uh, what about me? My magic woke up not too long ago." Jason doesn't look happy about going out to see the swamp creatures. I don't want to ever see them again, either, but I have to. If I don't, they'll keep hurting people.

"Your magic is wild right now, and you haven't learned to control it. You might do more harm than good." Alesha stands. "We should go to the hotel and get settled. Then we'll need a ride to the bayou."

"You'll be staying here."

"That's not…"

"Yes, it is necessary." Ezekiel cuts Sabien off. "My home is warded against everything, including the vampire stalking my daughter. You're safer here than at a hotel where he can get to you. I also have a large supply of dead man's blood. Do you?"

Sabien blinks. "No."

"Jameson!" Ezekiel calls, and the man comes in mere seconds later. "Can you show our guests to their rooms, please?

I'll tell Mrs. Banks to have a late supper ready, as we'll be going out to the swamp."

"Very good, sir." Jameson waits while we all stand then leads us upstairs. "All your luggage has already been placed in your rooms."

These people are pushy. I'm still not sure if we agreed to stay here, even though we're following the butler upstairs.

"Here you are, Miss Walker. I've put your and Mr. Rinaldi's luggage beside the bed."

"You knew Aleric was staying in my room?"

He only nods, his expression giving nothing away. Damn, these people do know a lot.

Once we're alone, Aleric pulls me to him. "I doan like dis, *Draga*, not one bit."

"I'm not sure I do, either, but this place is warded in ways we could never ward a hotel room. We're safer here."

"I can handle my bro'der."

I'm not so sure he can handle Kristoff, but I keep that to myself.

"Let's just rest for a little while, okay? I need all the strength I have to go and face that island again."

He kisses my forehead, and I snuggle against him on the bed, determined to try to forget about what's coming for just a little longer.

I always knew I'd be back here one day. I only hoped it would be years and years from now. Fate—or in this case, one sociopathic vampire—has other ideas. He probably already knows we're here. Kristoff isn't stupid. He's been around for hundreds of years and has learned to perfect the art of evil. He knows how to use humans to get what he wants, to protect him while he sleeps, and for his own sick, twisted amusements. He scares me more than I care to admit.

Aleric has told me a lot of stories about his time with Madame and his vampire family. This haunted look enters his eyes when he talks about Kristoff, and I know deep in my heart Madame used Kristoff to punish Aleric. I want so badly to take his pain away, to make him forget all that, but I can't. I can only try to give him new memories to combat all the horrible ones like he's done for me.

We pull up to a dock I recognize. It's the same one Sabien brought me to when I first came to New Orleans. Madame lived on an island in the middle of the swamp accessible only by boat. I'd been terrified that day, the same as I am today, only for different reasons. My Necromancy had just woken up, and I'd unknowingly pulled my dead dog from the ground. I woke up to him in bed beside me. He accompanied Sabien and me here so I could put him back where he belonged.

I did it easily, and that was perhaps the beginning of the end for me. Madame saw how much raw power I had. She wanted it, craved it, and would have killed me if not for Aleric's bravery. I owe him my life.

The same redneck as before steps out, shielding his eyes against the bright sun.

His beard hangs to his belly, the stringy hair full of things I don't want to think about. Bubba. That's his name. He doesn't look any happier to see us today than he had then.

Ezekiel brings the car to a stop and gets out, Sabien and Alesha right behind him. Aleric pulls me close, and I sit where I am. I don't need to talk to Bubba. The longer I can pretend I'm not here, the better off I'll be.

"You doin' okay, *bon fille*?" Aleric's Cajun is thicker today. He's just as terrified as I am.

"No." There isn't any point in lying to him. He'd smell it if I did. Vampires are funny like that.

"Me ei'der."

Reaching up, I cup his face and pull it to me, pressing my lips lightly to his. "I'm not going to let anyone hurt you ever again."

He smiles. "Dat be my job, *ma petite sorcière de la mort*."

My little death witch. He called me that my first day here. It was an insult then, but not anymore. It's an endearment now.

"How about we agree to take care of each other, then?"

"I can do dat." His lips brush mine again, but we're interrupted by raised voices. Turning, we see Sabien in a shouting match with the redneck. Ezekiel is standing with his arms crossed, looking bored.

"What's that about?"

"If I know Bubba, he doan want to go anywhere near dat island."

"Well, we have to get there. He's the only one who knows how."

Looking resigned, Aleric gets out, taking my hand to help me out of the car. Together, we walk the short distance to where they're shouting. As soon as Bubba sees Aleric, he stops talking. He looks shocked.

"Dey be a problem here, Bubba?"

Bubba crosses himself and turns to run back toward his shack, but Aleric is so much faster. I never even saw him move. It was more like I felt the air shift instead. He's leaning against the front door of the shack when Bubba skids to a stop.

"Do we have a problem?"

His voice is scary. The hairs on my arms rise, and I shudder away from the icy cold in his voice. His eyes flash red, and Bubba stutters something incoherent.

"You will take us to de island, Bubba, or you'll deal wit' me."

Bubba nods and trips over his own two feet in his haste to get away from my boyfriend. What the hell did Aleric do to cause this kind of fear? It's the same kind of fear Kristoff inspires in me.

Ezekiel is watching Aleric, a very calculated expression on his face. I don't like it.

"Come." Aleric takes my hand and leads me toward the boat that still appears to be on its final legs. The thing is a rust bucket begging to die.

We get onto the boat and take our seats. No life jackets in sight. Aleric pulls me into his lap and holds on tight. He won't look me in the eye. Not a good sign.

No one speaks as we pull into the water, and the hum of the old engine drowns everything out. I stare unseeingly at the trees on either side of us as we travel over the murky swamp. Memories of this ride flow through my mind. My dead dog sitting beside me, the stink unbearable, but washing my fingers through the wire of his carrier. He was afraid and trusted me to make it all better. Only I couldn't because he was dead. All I could do was put him back to rest.

The boat slows, and I force my thoughts away from those memories. It's darker here, the sun fighting to break through the overhead branches of the weeping willows that are so thick, it's hard to find purchase for the flimsy rays. The bayou is a place full of death and danger, its smell that of rot and decay.

But for me? It smells like the sweetest bouquet of flowers, calling to the Necromancy running through my veins. The scent is heady and one I could easily get drunk on. I use Alex's trick and dig my fingernails into my palms to make sure I don't do just that. Necromancers almost always turn evil because their gift is dark magic—blood magic—and as Aleric told me once, I may not want that to happen, but it will. I fight every day to make sure it doesn't, but it's a fear that lives inside me.

"Easy, *Draga*." Aleric's nose brushes mine as he leans in. "You're safe."

"I'm always safe with you." It's the one constant besides my bestie that I can count on. Aleric will sacrifice everything to keep me safe, and I'd do the same for him.

He winks, but he can't hide how nervous he is. He's as terrified of this place as I am. I lace my fingers with his. "We'll keep each other safe, yeah?"

"Always, *bon fille*."

It's the rare occasion he actually uses my name and only when he needs to make a point or show me how serious he is. It's always his Cajun slang or his nickname for me. *Draga*. I'm still not sure what that means, but I love it. It reminds me of dragons, and anyone who knows me knows I am a dragon fanatic. I rooted for the dragons in *Game of Thrones* instead of the people.

We turn the corner, and I see the dock that leads to the house. It's empty. No boats reside there like before. The whole place feels empty.

"Don't go near the dock." Alesha stands and goes to the front of the boat by Bubba. "Something's off."

"It feels empty," I tell her and go stand by her, Aleric beside me. "Which is weird because I can smell the death all around us."

"Are you sure it's de creatures you be smellin'?" Aleric asks softly. "Maybe it's just de normal dead t'ings you smell?"

"I will never forget what those things smell or feel like." A full body shudder wracks me. The slime zombies cause severe pain when they melt all over you. I'm not likely to forget that.

"My daughter told me the creatures can rob you of thought with the amount of pain their touch brings."

"One touched her?"

Ezekiel nods. "She's a hunter, much to my dismay. She came out here with her friend looking for a missing hunter. They found her floating in another body of water, and those creatures came after them. They touched her bare skin."

Maybe my initial thoughts about his daughter were wrong. If she's a hunter, it means she faces the supernatural all the time. Most hunters do good work, protecting the innocent. I should probably reserve my judgment for when I meet her. Assuming things about people almost always gets you into trouble. Doesn't mean we don't still do it, though.

"Maybe Aleric's right." Alesha rubs her arms absently. "It can't be empty of the creatures and you still smell them."

"It can, though." I close my eyes and find the bright light that is my magic and reach out toward the depths of the swamp, my magic seeking the creatures I know as well as I know my own body. They're there, but they're not responding. It's like they're frozen or something.

"*Draga?*"

I ignore Aleric and push my magic into them, calling to them, coaxing them to wake up and listen.

"Something's wrong."

"What?" Alesha leans over and looks into the murky water, which is silent except for the ripples caused by the motor of our boat.

"They're there. More than I can easily count, but it's like they're sleeping or frozen in place. Not even my magic can wake them, and it should do that if nothing else."

"Not if they're spelled." Alesha's lips thin. "From what you've told me of them, they'd already been tampered with to cause them to ooze and melt. Only dark magic can do that. It can also leave them susceptible to other spellcasters. This Kristoff may have hired a powerful witch to cast an ownership spell upon them."

"What's that?"

"Simply put, they only answer to one master for as long as the spell binds them." Ezekiel looks as upset as Alesha. "I'm guessing the moment we step foot on the island or shortly after, they'll come to life. That's what happened to the hunters who have tried to breach this island. Three have died in the process."

"I need to be able to get a feel for the magic that was used to create the binding spell." Alesha leans farther over the rail, trying to see beneath the cloudy waters.

"Can you do that thing Alex does where she holds your hand and you can see what she does?"

Alesha frowns. "No. That is something unique to her."

"I tol' you we shou' have brought her wit' us," Aleric all but growls as he moves away from the railing. A shiver rolls over him. He hates being here. Knowing those things are down there, just waiting to wake up and attack...I don't much like it, either.

"It wouldn't have helped because she can't touch me." Damn vampire backlash. I wish she hadn't absorbed so much of Aleric's vampirism, but then no one can explain why I can touch him and not her. Alesha said it makes no sense. She's been trying to find a work-around for over a year. I was hoping she could have held her mother's hand while I held Alesha's. I'm not sure it would have worked, anyway.

"Are you from around here?" Ezekiel asks, studying Aleric a little too closely.

"He lived here for a long while," I answer before Aleric can. "He picked up the dialect."

There are still questions on the tip of his tongue, but I don't want him focusing on my boyfriend. No one who doesn't already needs to know he's a vampire.

"I don't know how to show you the magic, then. Without Alex's help, I'm not sure what else to do other than to wake them up."

"That might be a little too dangerous for the moment." Ezekiel cups the back of his neck and squeezes. "Those things have killed seasoned hunters. And while you are a Necromancer, they're spelled. We don't know if your magic is strong enough to overcome the spell. Without an arsenal of weapons, I'm not willing to risk all our lives. We can come back tomorrow morning with a plan."

"Agreed." Alesha nods, still staring down into the waters. "I just wanted to get a feel for the magic that was used so I could start a plan to counter it, but I'm not willing to risk our lives, either. Tomorrow will be soon enough. I still think we should go to the hotel, though."

"Given what happened yesterday, I

don't think that's wise. There's more than enough room for everyone to stay at the plantation."

"What happened?" Alesha asks.

"There was an attempt on my daughter's life. I believe it was engineered by Kristoff. A bomb was sent to her fiancé's apartment. Had it not been for the quick thinking of Daniel, they might all be dead right now. I want everyone where I know I can keep you safe. As I said before, my home is warded against things you haven't even thought of."

"Including vampires?" I ask.

"Of course."

My gaze shifts to Aleric. His warding must not be too good because Aleric walked right through it. Alesha shakes her head slightly, and I stop the questions. Maybe she worked some kind of extra protection against wards into the talisman. Or maybe it's because his heart beats now. I'll ask her later.

"We're more than capable of defending ourselves." Alesha leans against the rail, her eyes almost glowing with her wolf. I don't think she even realizes it, but Ezekiel does. He takes a step back, his breath almost a gasp, but he recovers quickly.

"I'm sure you are, but why take chances when you don't have to? Besides, everyone's already settled into your rooms at home. No point in having to haul your luggage back downstairs."

"He's right." Aleric wraps his arms around me, his chin settling on the top of my head. "Kristoff is…you doan wan' to underestimate him. He's lethal and capable of t'ings you cain't even imagine."

Alesha studies him and nods after a moment. Whatever expression he's wearing must have been convincing. "My main priority is all of your safety, and if Mr. Crane can better provide that than the hotel, and if you're sure you're comfortable staying there, then that's what we'll do."

"I think we should." Hell, at this point, I'd agree to anything to get away from here. My skin has a surface memory of what it felt like to be covered in their slime, the pain eating away at my sanity. I shudder, and Aleric's arms tighten around me.

"Then it's settled." Ezekiel turns back to Bubba and instructs him to take us back to the dock. He doesn't waste time in turning the boat around.

I can't take my eyes away from the water as we speed away. Those things are down there, sleeping, waiting. Maybe I could have pulled them from their sleep, maybe I could have tasted their magic, but the truth is I'm afraid. The memory of those things still haunts me, and I'm scared I'll freeze up and let them hurt someone.

I need to figure a way to get around my own fear before we come back here. I settle against Aleric, who's watching the shoreline with the same intensity I am, and we're both quiet as we head back.

He doesn't want to face them or Kristoff any more than I do, but neither of us has a choice, unfortunately. I only hope we survive it this time.

Emma

It's late by the time we get back to Zeke's. We'd snuck out this morning, and I'd fended off the lecture last night by telling him I was tired and sore. Truth was I slept like the dead and snuck out like a thief in the night this morning with Mary, Eric, and Ethan, leaving Nathaniel and Dan sleeping. We went back to the apartment to try to sort through the main room. The bedrooms were fine, but I had a lot of pictures in the living room. Pictures I'd taken over the last couple of years that meant a lot to me. Unfortunately, most of them were ruined, including the one of me and Dan standing on Biloxi Beach from our first summer here in New Orleans. It was my favorite. It's only about an hour and half from the city, so I hope we can go again this summer and replace the pictures I lost.

"You ready to face your dad?" Mary asks as I pull into the drive. "He's been blowing up your phone."

"We should have been back two hours ago," Eric grouches. He's not at all happy about me trying to pretend Kristoff isn't the threat he is. I don't want my life controlled by fear, though. It's not in me to cower. I was always the girl who hit first and asked questions later. No matter how much I've grown from that foster girl, she's still very much a part of me.

"We're here before dark." Ethan leans up, his shoulders barely fitting through the console. He's buffed up since he's been working out with Eric, who's on the football team at school. "Weren't those people from West Virginia supposed to be here today?"

I close my eyes and lean my forehead on the steering wheel. "I forgot." Zeke is gonna kill me.

"You had a lot on your mind, Mattie." Mary is always the first one to reassure me. "Zeke will understand."

"Can we go inside before it gets dark?" Eric is more than a little grouchy. He sounds downright hostile.

"You didn't have to come if you didn't want to," I remind him, just as snarky as he is.

He huffs. "Who else is gonna keep you from getting yourself killed, Hathaway? Certainly not you since you can't get yourself inside before darkness falls."

"Awesome movie," Ethan mutters.

"Dude…"

"Chill, man. We're here. No harm, no foul. Everyone's safe."

The soothing tone in Ethan's voice seems to help calm Eric a little, but not by much. His blue eyes are snapping with anger. I know he thinks I'm taking too many chances, but I'm not. I'm drinking the nasty dead man's blood to keep Kristoff out of my dreams, and I'm home by dark. I know he's a threat. Heck, he might even have sent a bomb to Dan's apartment. I know this. I'm not doing anything stupid. Mostly.

Eric opens the rear door and gets out, slamming it behind him and stomping up the steps. Okay, so maybe he's not as calm as I thought.

"What is his problem?" I ask as he goes inside the house.

"He's worried." Ethan sits back, his own gaze on the door Eric disappeared through. "You and Mary are the closest thing he has to family, and the thought of losing you is freaking him out. Kristoff already got to you once while we were all right there in the hospital, while *Eric* was just a few feet away from your door."

"That wasn't his fault."

"He doesn't see it that way. He's got in his head that he's your protector. Said something about looking out for you even before you knew about it."

"Eric and I have a complicated history, one that's not up to me to tell you about," I say when I see the questions start to tumble out of him. "He'll tell you about it when he's ready."

"Did the two of you date or

something?"

"No." I take a deep breath, my hands flexing on the steering wheel. "I think we both had a crush at one time, and he did kiss me, but that was a long time ago."

"You kissed him?"

I glance in the mirror and note the anger on his face.

"It was a long time ago, Ethan, and he's family now. My brother."

His lips thin. "Are you sure he knows that?"

Enough is enough. They might both be pissed, but I'm done watching this dance. It's starting to irritate me.

"Ethan…"

"I think we all need to go inside before it gets any darker." Mary stops my tirade before I can start, giving me a warning glare. We'd agreed to let the two of them figure out their own feelings. Telling them could cause one or both to run scared. Neither of us wants that. I just wish they'd hurry up and admit how they feel. I know something happened over Christmas because they're both less weird, but I'm not sure what.

"Fine, let's go meet the witches." Before I get out, I turn to Ethan. "I swear to you, Eric and I are family, brother and sister. Dan is my whole world, and Eric is my best friend. That's all."

Ethan nods, his lips no longer smashed together in that thin line. "Sorry. I don't know what came over me."

"Yes, Ethan, you do if you'll just admit it." Before Mary can snark at me or Ethan can deny it, I get out of the car. I never said I wouldn't push them a little. Nothing wrong with a good kick in the rear.

The house is not quiet when I go inside. Voices come from the parlor, and I head that way. Eric is just outside the doorway, listening. He does that a lot. I think it's a leftover ghost thing. He was a ghost for a long time before I reaped his soul and put it back in the body of my ex-boyfriend, Jake Owens. Now Eric has a family, and Mr. and Mrs. Owens have one of their sons back. Sort of.

I lean against the wall beside him, my shoulder resting against his arm. He's taller than I am, but most people are since

I'm a short girl at barely five-three.

"I'm sorry."

He snorts, a habit he got from me. "No, you're not."

"I'm sorry you're mad at me."

His blue eyes peep down at me. "Why do you always have to do things that get you in trouble?"

"Because I'm me, and I'm always doing things I shouldn't. It's part of my charm."

"Charm, my ass."

I gasp. "You owe the swear jar a dollar!"

He laughs. "What are we going to do with all the money in your swear jar this month?"

"Donate it to the homeless shelter or maybe to the local children's hospital. Get the kids some new toys or something."

"It's hard to stay mad at you, Hathaway."

"That's because you love me." I grin at him, and he shakes his head, kissing my forehead.

"You *do* know I love you, right?"

"I know, Eric." I turn and hug him as tightly as I can. "I hate when you're mad at me."

He sighs. "It's a job not being mad at you, but you're my family, and I'll always do right by you."

"So, you're not mad at me anymore?" I ask hopefully.

"No, Mattie, I'm not mad at you anymore."

"Good." I hug him one more time before turning him loose, hearing the door open. "Love you, too."

Ethan gives me a hesitant smile, but he's not glaring anymore. Mary must have said something to calm him down. His jealousy could turn out to be a good thing for him and Eric. I hope so, anyway.

"Knock-knock," I call as Eric and I enter the room full of strangers. Beautiful strangers, at that. Not one of them looks like a normal individual. They could all be models, especially the guys. They could grace the pages of *GQ* magazine without blinking. Are all supernatural people just naturally beautiful or something? It always makes me feel self-conscious, as I don't think I'm beautiful despite what Dan says. I'm just me.

"Emma…"

"Sorry, Papa. I was at the apartment looking to see if any of my photos survived. I had these guys with me so I wasn't alone, and we're home before dark."

"Just barely," he snaps, pissed. I knew he would be.

"Are you going to introduce me?" I remind him of his manners, hoping to distract him.

His lips thin, understanding my tactic, but his manners take priority. He then rambles off everyone's names, pointing as he goes along the line of people sitting on the sofas and chairs. I wasn't expecting anyone but the Necromancer.

"And this is my daughter, Emma Crane." My papa, like the rest of us, never gives our full names. I understand his hesitancy here with so many witches. There is power in your name. Best not to give it out, as a rule.

"Hi. Nice to meet all of you. Who's the

Necromancer?"

"Me." The only blonde in the room holds up her hand. She's snuggled against the broody-looking model. The difference between them is like night and day. That's a good analogy. He's the darkness to all her sunshine.

"Glad to have you here. We need the help."

"Your dad took us out to the house. We're going to need some time to work through the spell on the dead in the water."

"Nasty things." My leg shudders, remembering the pain their touch caused.

The blonde nods. I don't remember her name, but I don't want to ask her, either. Mary's good with names. I'll ask her later.

"This is my sister Mary and my brothers, Eric and Ethan." I point them out one by one, and the group frowns, their curious gazes swinging back to Zeke. "We sort of adopted each other."

That makes sense to them.

"Did Papa fill you all in on the psycho stalker vampire?"

"He did, but I already know Kristoff. Madame, the Necromancer who used to live there, was my first teacher. She was just as crazy as the psycho vampires."

"Vampires? There's more than one?" How did we not know this?

"Dey were t'ree vampire bro'ders." The beautiful man speaks, his voice deep and sure and *very* Cajun. But there's something else there. It doesn't sound exactly like Cass's Cajun. It's more like a different accent buried beneath the bayou slang.

"Alice said there was only one there," I murmur. Three. Well, dang. How the heck will we deal with all those monsters in the water and three vampires if she was wrong?

"She's righ'," Mr. Gorgeous says. "Two have gone, and only Kristoff remains."

"How do you know?"

"That's not important." The older woman stands. She resembles the dark-haired girl by the other gorgeous man who looks like the guy sitting beside the Necromancer. Brothers, maybe?

Anyway, the boy sitting beside the girl with the stunning green eyes and mocha skin could be the dark-haired girl's brother, too. They do look more like the man than the woman, though.

"Yes, yes, it is." I don't like having half answers. It'll get you killed if you don't know the whole truth. I've learned that while hunting. "If you want us to trust you, then you have to tell us the truth. I'm not dying because you lot weren't truthful with us."

The woman's brown eyes narrow.

"My daughter's right. You can either tell us or I'll find out on my own, and *I will find out*. It's easier if you decide to come clean now."

Come clean? Zeke's definitely picking up some of our sayings.

"We're here to hunt down a vampire and get rid of zombies. That's all you need to know." The woman has a no-nonsense attitude that really pisses me off.

"One thing I learned real quick is you have to trust the people around you when you're hunting. If you can't, people die.

I'm not taking any of you anywhere near there unless you tell me how you know the other two vampires aren't there. If you can't do that, sorry we wasted your time. I'm sure Papa can locate another Necromancer."

The woman regards me. I've stood up during my mini tirade without realizing it. Her eyes flicker with something like recognition, but that can't be right. I've never met her before.

"I understand you think you need to know, but you don't. I'm older and wiser…"

"You might be older, lady, but you ain't wiser. I survived foster care. I've faced down demons, roogies, ghosts, vampires, destroyed a Fallen Angel *and* a primordial evil. Don't sit here and be condescending to me, because it won't get you anywhere but out the front door."

Who the heck does she think she is coming in here acting like she knows everything?

"Rougarou," Ethan points out mildly.

"*What. Ever.*" I shoot him a glare hot enough to scorch Texas.

"Your eyes…" The dark-haired girl leans forward, her mouth open. "You have wolf eyes."

"And?"

"I didn't realize you were a shifter." She glances to the blond boy on her other side. He's leaning into her and sniffing the air. Honestly, I wonder if she's not dating both of them, the way she's surrounded by them. Weird.

"There's a lot you don't know about me."

"You smell like one of us, but you don't." Blondie sits up a little straighter.

"Are you sniffing me?"

He shrugs.

"That's rude, man." Ethan frowns. "Manners, people, manners."

The dark-haired girl looks mortified and elbows him in the ribs. Her other guy laughs.

"As entertaining as you are, are you going back to the airport or are you going to 'fess up?"

"What my daughter said." There's no mistaking the pride in my father's voice. He loves that I'm more like him every day. We both do what we have to do, even play dirty, to protect those we love. Neither of us will apologize for the things we do in that endeavor. And I sure as heck ain't letting these people get my family killed.

"It's fine." The guy wrapped around the Necromancer pulls her closer. "I was a prisoner of Madame's for many years before I escaped wit' Saidie. I fed de vampires dere. I know how many dey were and dat now only Kristoff remains."

He was forced to be chow for them? That's awful. "I'm sorry that happened to you."

He shrugs. "It is wha' it is, *chèr*."

"But how do you know that only Kristoff is left? What about the others? How do you know where they went?"

"Only Kristoff was a bad one. De od'ers, dey were as much victims of Madame as I was. Dey let me know when dey moved on."

"Why would they do that?" I'm more up to snuff on vampire lore now, but I don't know how vampire packs work. I'm not sure any hunter has ever let any den live long enough to ask about the inner workings of one.

"Saidie, she killed Madame, and dey wanted me to know dey were grateful to her for settin' dem free. Dey wanted her to know dey held no ill will toward her and wouldn't seek vengeance for killing dere mo'der."

Huh.

"Okay. That's all I wanted to know. I don't like people keeping secrets. It gets others killed if we don't know everything."

"I don't see how knowing that keeps you from getting killed," Alesha mutters so low almost no one in the room hears her, except for me and the other shifters.

"Because we now know Kristoff fed from him, and that opens his mind up to him. It makes him vulnerable, and it might lead to the psycho getting into his head and making him do something he normally wouldn't. Now that we know to be on the lookout for that, it'll be easier to counter, and no one will end up hurt trying to stop him from doing something Kristoff might coerce him into. *That's* why it's important."

She doesn't look too happy with my explanation, but I couldn't care less.

"In the spirit of full disclosure, he fed from me, too, but I'm chocked so full of dead man's blood, it's a moot point."

"Where's Daniel?" Zeke asks when no one else speaks.

"Working. They caught a case this morning. Where's my brother?"

"He said he had things to do."

That's it? That's all I get? "It's dark, Papa."

"Your brother can take care of himself."

Crap. I pull out my phone and text Nathaniel. He better be somewhere safe.

"He's fine."

"You thought I was fine too until a bomb got delivered to the apartment and almost blew us all up!" I swear by all that's holy, if anything's happened to my brother...

My phone chirps with an incoming text from Nathaniel saying he'll be here in a few minutes. Thank God.

"Papa, I love you, but if you let

something happen to my brother because you don't like him, I will never forgive you."

His nostrils flare when he sees I mean what I say. He starts to reply, but then his gaze flickers to our captive audience. "Jameson, why don't you show our guests to their rooms so they can get cleaned up for dinner? My kids and I need to have a conversation."

"Of course, sir."

Where the heck did Jameson come from? He wasn't here a second ago. He's sneaky like that, though.

Zeke waits until our guests are upstairs before he speaks.

"I was not willfully putting your brother in danger, Emma Rose. He's saved your life too many times for me to do that. He was raised in this life and has more protections than you do. He knows how to handle himself even against a psycho vampire, as you called Kristoff. If I didn't believe this, I wouldn't have let him leave this house today."

I honestly want to believe Zeke, but if something happened to Nathaniel, he wouldn't lose any sleep over it, either.

"Now, let's talk about you and your willingness to put yourself and everyone else at risk. It's dark, as you pointed out. You also almost got blown up, as you pointed out as well. Care to explain why you snuck out of the house this morning without telling a soul?"

He aims that at all of us. The others look properly chastised, but I'm not. They're reeling from him calling them his kids. I know Zeke considers all of us his, but I don't think they realized until just this second that they belong to him. They're his children, same as me. I'm betting it means more to Eric than it does to Mary or Ethan simply because Eric was a foster kid, too. We never had family growing up, and family is all a foster kid ever hopes to have.

"Do you understand how stupid that was?" Zeke snarls, his anger out in full force. "Daniel was livid, and he had every right to be."

I wince at that. I have an entire phone full of text messages along the same lines from Dan. He's pissed, but I just wanted to get away from here for a little while. I needed to process what happened, and the easiest way to do that was to go back to the scene of the crime. It's not like I went by myself. I had Mary, Eric, and Ethan.

"Your father's right. You could have gotten them all killed, Mattie Louise Hathaway."

My head swivels to see Silas leaning against the mantel of the fireplace. Zeke doesn't even get mad. He just shakes his head. Silas is a demon who also happens to be my grandfather. Zeke will never acknowledge the demon as family, but I do. He's saved my bacon more times than I can count. He loves me in his own way, and despite my fear of him, I love him, too.

He's also just as pissed as Dan and Zeke. He never uses the name I grew up with. It's always "Emma Rose" or "my darling girl." He only ever uses "Mattie" when he wants to get a point across.

"I was perfectly safe. We didn't take chances, and we got back before dark."

Eric makes a noise, and I shoot him a baleful glare.

"Just barely."

He had to do it, didn't he?

"You see? Even your brother thinks it was too dangerous." Zeke sounds vindicated.

When Eric doesn't disagree, I throw my hands up and fall on the couch that had just been vacated by our visitors.

"Traitor," I mouth at Eric.

He raises an eyebrow in retaliation.

Silas sniffs the air. "I smell wet dog."

"There are shifters in the house," Mary tells him and comes to sit by me. "We weren't expecting them, only the Necromancer."

"Well, that's a wrinkle." Silas's rich British accent is out on full display tonight. I've tried to mimic it, but I can't. "But that's not why I'm here."

"I was going to tell you about the bomb..."

"That's not why I'm here, although we will be having a discussion about that later." There's the hint of the promise of pain, and I shrink back. Silas has no qualms hurting me if he thinks it'll stop me from doing something stupid, but he should know by now that even pain doesn't do that. I end up doing epically stupid things anyway.

"Why are you here, then?" Zeke's got a tic in his forehead from the vein throbbing so hard there. He hates that Silas and I have such a close relationship.

"I have information for you on the boy's mother."

"Cass?" I perk up. Dan wasn't having any luck locating information on Cass's mother, so I asked Silas to look into it. He was curious enough not to demand something in return for the information.

"Why are you trying to find information on his mother?" Zeke asks, confused.

"Because he found out his dad wasn't really his dad, and he wants to know where he came from. Dan tried looking into it, but there's no information on her before Cass was born. He thought maybe witness protection, but there's more to it than that. Cass isn't quite human. He's something else."

Zeke pales, literally pales in front of us, and grabs the back of the chair to steady himself.

"Papa?"

"He's not a Willow?"

"No."

Silas laughs. "Oh, I did not expect this."

"What the heck are you two going on about?"

"She told me…" Zeke shakes his head, dazed. "She swore to me…"

Ethan and Eric exchange a look, both of them pushing off their respective walls to come sit with me and Mary.

What's going on?

"The boy's mother is an Angel. Fallen, but not a Fallen Angel."

"There's a difference?" Ethan asks.

Silas nods. "Fallen are those who fall from grace because they love a human. Fallen Angels are those that followed the Morning Star in the battle of Heaven and were banished to the darkest pits of Hell. Most of them were once Arch Angels."

"He's Nephilim?" Mary nods thoughtfully. "I guess that makes sense, in a way."

"It does?" I haven't moved my gaze

from my dad. Zeke looks ready to pass out.

"Think about it. Cass protects humans, looks out for them, which is an Angel's prime directive. He's also incredibly kind, something you'd associate with Angels."

Yeah, Mary and I have two different opinions on Angels. I've met one, and they are not all that kind, at least not the one I met.

"You're sure he's not a Willow?"

"Yeah, his uncle confirmed it for him, but he wouldn't tell him who his father is." I link my fingers with both Mary and Eric, seeking comfort. "What's wrong, Papa?"

"I…"

Silas cackles. Not laughs, not chuckles…he cackles.

"Papa?"

"He's mine."

And with that statement, Zeke turns and walks out of the room, leaving everyone but Silas reeling in shock.

After Zeke dropped that bombshell, he locked himself in his study and refused to let me in. Or anyone. I even broke down and called my grandmother Lila, explaining what happened. She came over, and he wouldn't open the door for her either. After that, she grilled me for over an hour on all I know about Cass Willow.

Dinner came and went, Mrs. Banks serving our guests in the dining room while the rest of us nibbled on something in the kitchen. Ethan and Eric are upstairs playing video games, and Mary's somewhere. I told her I needed time alone to think. She respected that.

Cass is my brother.

I'm not sure how to feel about that. I'm actually grossed out because I thought he was cute, and if I hadn't had Dan, I might have liked him. Thank God for small miracles.

I think about texting Dan, but this is news that needs to be delivered in person. He's always been a little jealous of Cass, especially because I'm forever putting myself squarely in danger to help him. He knows I wouldn't do that for just anyone. The first time I met Cass, I trusted him instinctively, but I thought it was because he reminded me of Eli. Not that Cass looks like Eli, but his mannerisms and wicked sense of humor and that charm…that's what made me think of Eli.

But that wasn't it at all. It was my mind trying to make sense of something I knew deep down. I recognized Cass because of Zeke. He has my father's blue eyes. The rest of the Willows have brown eyes, but not Cass. His are blue. He must get his blond hair from his mother.

He's my brother.

Cass is not going to be happy about this. He was raised to hate everything about the Cranes, thanks to his uncle. He's not like me and Zeke. He has morals. Not that I don't, I just don't mind breaking mine when necessary to protect the people I love. I'm not sure Cass would.

How am I going to tell him?

He accepts me because I wasn't raised to be a Crane. I grew up in foster care. If I'd grown up under my father's roof, Cass and I might even be enemies right now.

There's a knock on my door, and then it opens, revealing Nathaniel. He leans against the doorframe. "You okay?"

I shake my head.

"I saw your grandmother downstairs. She's as scary as my own grandmother, and that's saying something." He pushes off the door and comes to sit beside me. "She and Mary were talking, and I decided to come check on you."

"Lila loves Mary as much as she does me. Sometimes I think she wishes Mary was her granddaughter instead of me."

"What do you mean?"

"Mary is great with makeup and fashion and parties. She doesn't do or say things that embarrasses Lila in front of her friends. Lila actually winces when I talk sometimes."

"She loves you."

"I know, but that doesn't mean I don't embarrass her."

"I'm still thinking it was easier with Lila than it was with me."

"What do you mean?"

"You trust her."

"I mostly trust you."

He laughs. "I can't blame you. I outright admitted I came here to kill you and take your gifts."

"I'm still afraid if you discover everything I can do, you might."

"I know exactly who you are, Emma. I've known since the Rougarou attack."

He can't know.

"My grandma didn't raise no fool." His southern drawl is quite charming. "The moment I saw the goddess and the way she looked at you, I knew. There's no mistaking the way a parent looks at a child."

I gape at him.

"There's only one way to kill a Fallen Angel. It has to be the perfect trifecta of power—the power of creation, the power of death, and something to bind the two and bridge the gap. Gods and goddesses stopped having children long before the Greeks rose to power. There are those out there who have leftover, weakened blood in their genealogy from those gods and goddesses who walked the Earth, but to do what you did, it had to be a full-on, up-close-and-personal bloodline. Until I saw your mother, I tried to tell myself that demon found a way around it. But there is no way around it. Angels were made that way."

"Did knowing make you question your decision not to kill me?" I force the words out, afraid of the answer.

"No, not even a little." He wraps an arm around my shoulders, scooting closer. "The power I could gain for myself from your death is more power than any one person should be capable of, but the thought of hurting you is abhorrent to me. You're my sister, Emma. I love you."

I take a deep breath and focus on keeping it together. I didn't used to be a person who cried. Crying means weakness, and I'm not a weak person. You can't be weak in the system or you get run over; you get molested. Over the years, I've come to realize crying doesn't make you weak. It makes you human, and I'm so far from that anymore, any little reminder I still have a human soul means a lot to me.

"I didn't have anyone growing up," I say softly. "No one to look out for me but me. I didn't trust anyone. I couldn't. I didn't know how to love people or to let them love me. You didn't know that girl."

"But I do," he says just as softly. "I can still see her in the way you have a hard time trusting people. I see her when she looks at me and wonders if she's going to have to kill me to protect herself. I see her when she fights like a demon to keep those she loves safe. I see her every day."

"Really?"

"Really. And you know what else?"

"What?"

"I'm glad I didn't find you before I did because my grandparents would have murdered you and fed me your blood. It's who they are. I'd never have gotten to know you, let alone learn to love you. You're changing me in ways I didn't expect and sometimes I'm not even sure I like. I put people before I do myself now, and that's not how I was raised. It never bothered me what anyone would think of me, but it does now. You and your family, their opinion matters."

"They're your family now, too."

His lips tilt. "It might take me a while to understand what that means aside from you. I've never had people who love me."

"Your grandparents love you."

"In their way, they do, but you don't teach someone to walk through life without a conscience and still say you love them the way you're supposed to love a child. I see the way your father and grandparents treat you, how they worry and want you to do good things. I never had that growing up."

"I'm so sorry, Nathaniel."

"So, in a way, you and I had a similar childhood. We grew up not understanding what real love is. We took what we wanted, and we didn't worry too much about the consequences."

"I never thought about it like that before." It's mind-blowing when you think of it that way. We were both lost little kids who didn't know better. "If it hadn't been for Dan, I'd still be like that. He taught me what love was."

"You did that for me."

"I did?"

"You did, and as uneasy as it makes me, I think it's a good thing. I'm learning to be a better person."

"I think so, too. None of that means we won't do what we have to, though."

"Very true, little sister, very true." He kisses my temple. "Now, do I still have a room to sleep in, or are all these people from West Virginia finally encroaching on your father's massive number of bedrooms?"

"I'm not sure I like that woman very much."

"Why not?"

"She was condescending to me, acting like she knew better just because she's older. Even Zeke knows not to pull that crap with me. It gets you nowhere fast."

"One of the first things your father should have taught you is that older people in the supernatural community tend to think they do know better than everyone else, especially those of us who they think are still wet behind the ears. I'm not shocked she acted like that, especially given who she is."

"Wait, you know them?"

"Their names are famous in the magical community. The Blackburnes are as old as we are with a heritage just as messed up. Alesha Blackburne and her brother Sabien are several hundred years old."

"What?" I screech, unable to help myself.

Nathaniel laughs. "They're witches, and witches live long lives, as long as shifters do."

"Holy cow. How long do shifters live?"

"Oldest one I know of is around three thousand years old."

My mouth drops open. No freaking way!

"There is so much to teach you. We need to get you up to snuff on the three main magical Families of Power, two of which are residing under your roof right now."

"My head hurts."

"I know it's a lot."

"Did you ever just want to be normal?"

"When I was little and I saw how happy all my friends were, I wished I could be more like them. I wanted to go to picnics and pool parties and sleepovers, but when you're a Dubois, that's not in the cards. Grandmother stamped that out before it even got started."

"I'm sorry."

He shrugs. "We can't change our past, Emma. We can only move forward and try to be better."

"I didn't get to do any of that, either. Maybe we should do it now."

"Do what now?"

"Have pool parties and picnics and sleepovers."

He laughs. "I think we have the sleepovers down."

"Yeah, I guess we do." I bump his shoulder with mine. "I love you, Nathaniel. You know that, right?"

"You do?"

"I do. As much as I do Zeke and Lila and Josiah and Mary and Eric and Ethan. Took me a little while to get there because I was afraid of you. I'm not anymore, though."

"Good, because I love my baby sister, too."

For the first time since meeting him, I feel like he's my brother and he'll protect me. I should have talked to him a lot sooner.

"What are we gonna do about Cass?"

"Cass?" He frowns. "What about him?"

"No one told you?"

"I'm *persona non grata* in this house, short stuff. No one tells me squat."

"He's my brother."

"Come again?"

"Like flesh and blood brother, same as you. Zeke is holed up in his office refusing to talk to anyone. From what little he said, I think Cass's mom lied to him when he asked her about it. He's in a little bit of shock. That's why Lila's here. She came to try to talk him down off the ledge and get him to come out of his office."

"Shock isn't the word I'd use. He has a son who hates him and grew up learning to take him out. He's in a little more than shock."

"You think Cass really hates him?"

"Probably."

Nathaniel has never lied to me. He and Silas are the only two men in my life I can say that about. I hope to God he's wrong, though. It'll kill Zeke if his son hates him.

"You think he'll hate me when he finds out?"

"No, Emma, I don't. He knows you, and he already loves you. Finding out you're his sister will not push him away but will bring him closer to you. And if that's not the case, I'll beat his ass."

"Swear jar!"

He filches a dollar out of his pocket and hands it over. "You're the only person I know who doesn't cuss."

"You don't have to cuss to get your point across."

"I'm not saying it's a bad thing. It makes you unique and one of many reasons the people around you love you."

"Thanks for not murdering me."

"Thanks for giving me a chance."

I hug him and receive another gift. That same feeling when I hug Zeke filters in, that feeling of warmth and love and family. It took a while, but what I told Mary earlier is true. Nathaniel isn't just my brother, he's family.

"Hey, can I ask you a question without you getting mad at me?"

"I won't promise not to get mad or to answer, but I promise to hear you out."

"You've been around lawyers too much recently," he says wryly.

That's true enough. Between setting up The Hathaway Foundation and learning more about Zeke's businesses, I've been swimming in lawyers.

"It's about Mary."

Instantly, I'm cautious. My sister has been through more than most people should ever have to survive in a thousand lifetimes.

"Why does she limp?"

"Have you asked her?"

"No. I get the feeling it would cause her pain, and I don't want to do that."

"You like my sister, don't you?"

He sighs. "She's too good for me, Emma. I don't deserve someone who is at her core a better soul than anyone I've ever met, and that's what Mary is. She's not tainted like we are. She's full of light and joy, even when I see the depths of the pain in her eyes. Not even that can wipe away how good she is."

He's right about that. Mary is a soul not meant for this Earth. She belongs in Heaven with the Angels. I knew that a long time ago, but I'm selfish, and I want her here with me for as long as I can keep her.

"I think the only person who should judge who is good enough for Mary is Mary." Not saying I'm okay with

Nathaniel even trying to get close to Mary, because he is a Dubois. He's as dark at his core as I am, but that decision isn't mine to make. It's Mary's.

Besides, I saw how he was with her at the apartment when the bomb went off. He protected her both from the blast and everything that came later. They may fight like cats and dogs, but I think maybe there's something there worth exploring, and I'm not one to judge and stand in the way of Mary finding what Dan and I have.

But there's Caleb. Mary really loves Dan's brother even though he broke her heart. I can't blame Caleb for choosing to stay with his family after Eli died, but Mary needed him, too. Sometimes it doesn't matter how much we love someone or how understanding we are of their choices and why they made them. Sometimes love really isn't enough, and I'm afraid that's the case with Mary and Caleb. I could be dead wrong, but no one knows that but Fate.

"Do you remember me telling you about Mrs. Olsen and how Mary and I were both her prisoners?"

He nods.

"She tortured Mary for weeks before I found her. She put scars on her body that won't heal. Zeke's had every specialist he can find look at her, but the damage to her leg was severe. She'll have a limp for the rest of her life. Her leg hurts her sometimes, but she tries not to let on. If I could figure out this healing thing, I'd heal her myself. It's the least I could do after she took me in and accepted me for who I was when I was still running from myself."

"I...I never knew. I know you said y'all were held captive, but I didn't know torture was involved. Even for you?"

I nod. "She smashed my hands. It took four surgeries to get them to a point where they started to look normal. I'd still not be able to use them if Silas hadn't healed them."

"That demon loves you, doesn't he?"

"In his own way, as best as he can, yeah. Same as your grandparents do you."

"No, it's not the same. I can't define

160

how it's different, but I know it is."

I can't even argue because he knows his grandparents better than I do.

"Just promise me one thing, Nathaniel."

"What's that?"

"Don't hurt her. She's been hurt more than anyone should ever have to be, and she's just starting to come around to your charm."

"I'll do my best."

"Do better than your best, or I'll have to throw down, and Mattie Louise Hathaway has never lost a fight. I don't fight fair."

"Of that, I have no doubts."

"Come on, let's go find you a place to sleep."

My brother gets up and follows me out into the hallway, and no matter how wrong everything is right now, it's also pretty danged right.

After finding my brother a makeshift bedroom, I see a text come in from Dan saying he's probably not going to be home tonight. They caught a bad case. I've gotten so used to being next to him at night, I'm not sure how I'm supposed to go to sleep. Not like I could anyway with everything on my mind. I do, however, text Cass and ask him to come over. But he says he can't get here until tomorrow. He and his cousin Robert are dealing with a haunting in a group home run by an old lady his uncle knows several hours out of the city.

Ethan and Eric are talking. Mary is FaceTiming her mom, and Nathaniel said he had some stuff to do on his laptop.

Which leaves me with nothing to do.

I go upstairs and knock on the Necromancer's door instead of twiddling my thumbs. We didn't really talk much earlier, and I want to get a feel for her. What I've read on Necromancers isn't all that comforting. They tend to be one of the evilest supernatural creatures there is.

I have to make sure I can trust my family around her.

The guy who'd been wrapped around her opens the door. He stares me down, and I stare right back at him. Scarier people than him have tried that game and lost.

"Wha' you wan'?" he asks after a long minute.

"Can I come in and talk?"

He looks behind him then shrugs, moving aside so I can enter. The blonde girl is sitting in the window bench with the dark-haired girl from before. The guy I think is his brother sits on the bed. They all look at me expectantly.

"Hey, I don't think we got off on the right foot before. I have issues with authority, and when I think someone's holding back information that could keep my family safe, I tend to get snarky. I thought maybe we could start over?"

The dark-haired girl smiles. "Sure, we'd like that. I'm Alex. This is my boyfriend Luca, and this is Saidie and her boyfriend, Aleric."

"Aleric? Get out!"

Aleric's eyebrows furrow. "Som'tin wrong wit' mah name?"

"No. It's just that my brother's name is Aleric."

"Really?" Alex asks, a grin starting to tip the corners of her mouth up. "That's cool."

"I'm Emma. Can I sit?" I gesture to the bed where Mr. Broody sits, as I've dubbed him. Alex's boyfriend does not look approachable. He looks like he'd rather I do anything but sit on the bed with him. Tough. It's my father's house, and I'll sit where I please.

I plop down on the bed. "Sorry about before. That woman got on my last nerve, and I reacted badly. I tend to lash out, and my not-so-nice side comes out when I get mad. Bad habit."

"She's Alex's mom," Saidie says, pulling her legs under her Indian style.

"Man, I keep sticking my foot in it, don't I?"

Alex laughs. "She's not my favorite person, either. My mom and I are trying to get to a better place than we are, but it takes time."

"Well, at least your mom didn't try to murder you. Two of mine did, and one abandoned me. I think I have you beat in the deadbeat moms department." Everyone goes quiet and looks horrified. "TMI?"

"Maybe?" Saidie laughs.

"No, it just makes you and me kindred spirits." Alex's fists clench, and she winces. "My mom abandoned me and my brother when we were kids. She wiped my memory of an event that caused me to have some serious problems. I spent most of my teenage years convinced I was crazy and in a nuthouse. Sometimes I still wonder if I am crazy."

Luka gets up and has her in his lap in a heartbeat. "You are no *leerky, munya*.

You are here with me and your family."

She nods, but there's something in her expression that says she's still fighting to believe that.

"*Leerky*?" I've never heard that word before.

"It means crazy in Romani," Saidie explains.

"I don't mean to be insensitive, but if you're gonna have issues, I need to know. And not just to keep my family safe, but yours, too."

"My grandfather was obsessed with gaining power. He wanted mine, and to get it, he needed to consume my blood."

I nod. I know that much about gaining magical abilities.

"He put me into a trance, I guess you can say, where I found myself back at Compton Academy, the nuthouse I was telling you about. Everything made sense to me there. All the things I experienced here had a sane explanation there. Like when my magic woke up, it felt like my skin was crawling with thousands of bugs, and there I was coming down off all the meds they had me on."

"You were experiencing withdrawal symptoms."

"Which explained the buzzing and the crawling."

I get why she'd be confused.

"If it wasn't for Conner, our other friend with the purple eyes, I might not have ever found my way back here. He helped me. He brought my brother Jason there to that reality. This Jason loves me, and that Jason hated me. I can't be somewhere my brother hates me, so I chose this reality. I chose my family, I chose Luka, but sometimes, I still get glimmers of that other reality trying to break through, and I have to remind myself this is real. Even though maybe it's not."

Wow. Girl's got serious issues, but I get it. I don't think I could be somewhere the Mary who loves me wasn't. I wouldn't survive without her.

"Well, this is real. I'm real."

"You sure?"

"Given all the crap I've gone through in my life, I'm pretty sure."

"Well, I could have made up a

backstory for you in my head, and you'd never know the difference."

"We've gone over this, Alex. There's no way you'd ever make me wake up with my dead dog in my bed and Mom refusing to even look at me. You're not cruel."

"Trust me, if I thought that was true," I say, "I'd punch you right in the face, because I've been through some crap."

"Growing up here, it couldn't have been that bad," Saidie says, twisting a lock of her blonde hair.

"I didn't grow up here. I was kidnapped as a baby and ended up in foster care after my mom, or the woman who took me, tried to kill me. She did it to keep me safe, though. Took me years to come to terms with that. My birth mother, however, made a deal with a Fallen Angel to sacrifice me to him for a blood debt her family owed him. And my other mother, she walked away without even trying to understand who she was turning me over to. She walked out without any hesitation. That, I still haven't forgiven her for, but I'm working on it."

Saidie and Alex look at each other then burst into laughter. "You really do have us beat in the mom department." Alex shakes her head. "I didn't think I'd ever meet anyone with a more screwed-up past than me."

"Why your mama try to keep you safe by killing you?" Luka asks, his thumb rubbing slow circles on Alex's hand. Dan does that to me when he's trying to calm me down.

"She thought Zeke was a bad person who was going to murder me to take my powers, so she took me and ran. She knew about my gifts—or sorta, maybe. She was also trying to hide me from the demon who orchestrated my kidnapping, and I guess in her doped-up mind, the only way to protect me was to remove me from the situation. Only I didn't stay dead. When I woke up, so did my reaping abilities."

"Reapin'?" Aleric stands a little straighter where he's been leaning against the wall beside Saidie. "You're a livin' reaper?"

"I am."

"You hav' tah die to become one, dou…" His deep green eyes grow a little brighter. "Dat wha' you mean, den? When you said you didn't stay dead?"

"The EMTs were able to get my heart started again, and I woke up in the hospital seeing dead people at the ripe old age of five."

"Damn, that sucks." Saidie scrunches up her face in sympathy.

"You owe a dollar to the swear jar," I tell her.

"What's a swear jar?"

"I don't cuss, and I ask the people around me not to as well. When they do, they donate a dollar to the swear jar. We donate the money every month to one of the homeless shelters."

"You're weird."

"I know," I tell Saidie. "It's what makes me me."

"Do you really end up with a lot of money in that thing?"

"Oh, yeah. One month, Cass put so much money in it, it was enough to feed the shelter for the whole month."

"Seriously?"

I nod, laughing. "He tells me all the time I'm going to bankrupt him."

"Cass is…?"

"A hunter and my brother."

"But you said your brother's name was Aleric?"

"I have two blood brothers. My biological mother had another son, and Cass is my dad's son. We literally just found out he's a Crane tonight. Ethan and Eric are my brothers by choice."

"How…"

"Long story short, he found his family lied to him, and his dad wasn't his dad. He asked me and my fiancé for help, and the truth came out tonight in front of my dad. He said Cass's mom swore to him that Cass wasn't his, and he believed her. I haven't even told Cass yet. He hates the Cranes…well, except for me."

"Wow, no wonder you were snippy earlier. We didn't know you guys were dealing with all that."

I don't tell her that we found out later. I'll let her believe whatever she wants to believe.

"Just another day in my screwed-up, crazy life." I didn't mean to tell them any of that, but the girls are easy to talk to, and for me, that's huge. I'm guarded around new people, and that's not the case with these guys.

"So, you have a fiancé?" Alex asks after a minute, eyeballing my ring.

I hold my hand out for her to see. "His name's Dan, and he's a detective with the supernatural division of the New Orleans Police Department."

"You guys have your own spook squad?" Saidie's eyes go round. "That's cool."

"I'm a little worried about him. He's going to be out there in the dark with Kristoff tonight. After his apartment got bombed yesterday, I'm scared of what he'll do to Dan."

"Kristoff is no' one to be taken lightly." Aleric's expression darkens. "He takes pleasure in de pain of o'ders."

"Yeah, I got that when he broke my arm in the hospital to prove he could."

"He broke your arm?" Saidie looks at my arm. "When?"

"Couple days ago. It's healed now."

She arches a brow in question. "One of my grandfather's gifts is the ability to heal, and as soon as I got released from the hospital, he did just that."

"That'd be a cool grandpa to have around."

"He can be." No need for them to know Silas is a demon, either. I may find it easy to talk to them, but I'm not spilling the beans about everything. "That's what I came in here to talk to you about. I wasn't here when you arrived, so I don't know what you do and don't know."

"Kristoff is the only thing that scares me," Saidie says softly. "Even the Necromancer's curse didn't scare me as much as he does."

"The Necromancer's curse?"

"Madame was the only Necromancer Alex's uncle knew, and he asked her to train me when my gifts woke up. Only she decided she wanted my gifts for her own, but she couldn't kill me until I told her where to find Alex and Luka." Her eyes flicker to them. "I refused to tell her a thing even after she let those things in the water torture me for hours."

My leg flares at the memory of when one of them grabbed my bare skin. It's not something I'll ever forget, and Saidie suffered a lot longer than I did. "You were protecting the people you love."

She nods. "There's a spell that forces the souls of the dead to attack my aura until they break through and drive me crazy. Not insane, but truly crazy. Think of hundreds of schizophrenics and then quadruple that number. If it hadn't been for Alex's mom, I wouldn't have survived it."

"And Kristoff scares you more than that?"

"He's not just crazy, he's evil."

"I know. I saw it in his eyes. He's serial killer evil. And he's decided I'm his new plaything since I took Alice away from him."

Alex takes a ragged breath. "He no get near you, *munya*. You're safe. I swear it."

"Are you two brothers or something?" I ask.

Saidie laughs. "Yeah, they are."

"It's just that—and no offense—but you don't sound like each other. Luka's English is broken, and he has a different accent than you do. You sound like Cass, but your Cajun is different."

"My brother was given to the Necromancer when our mother refused to do the bidding of the witches." Luka's expression hardens, and I flinch away from him. Yeah, no, Kristoff has nothing on this guy. I think he could kill with no conscience.

"Why would you have to do the bidding of the witches, though? Did you owe them?"

"We are Romani, Gypsy," Luka says. "My people were and still are slaves to the witches."

Slaves? "That's awful."

"And another reason my mother and I are not close. She looks at Luka as less than human. To her, he's just a slave, and he's not. He's my mate." Her wolf flares in her eyes as she gets agitated. This is a touchy subject for her.

"No offense, but I knew there was a reason I didn't like that woman."

"None taken." Alex shrugs and buries herself into Luka. "I already told her if she can't accept him, she and I are done. I miss the mother I remember from when I was a little girl, and I want to try to rebuild our relationship, but not at the expense of my mate."

"You're both shifters, then? I didn't think witches could be shifters. Or maybe I'm wrong. I'm still pretty new to this whole supernatural world, outside of ghosts."

And just like that, scary Luka comes out to play. His eyes go onyx with red rings where his irises should be. His face morphs into something not quite human.

"You will tell no one of that secret."

"Dude, chill. I have no reason to go blabbing when I have my own secrets to protect."

"That go for every one of your people. If they blab, as you say, they will no see me coming. And when I am done, no one lives."

Crap on toast, he's freaking scary. Silas scary. But no one threatens my family. No one.

"You don't know who I am or what I can do. I killed a freaking Fallen Angel, so do not think you can threaten me. I'll take you apart piece by piece if you so much as sneeze in my family's direction."

"Holy shit," Saidie whispers. "Her eyes."

They're probably demon black.

"They look like yours, Luka."

"Like I said, you don't know me or what I can do, so I'd keep the threats to yourself."

"I think everyone needs to take a step back and calm down." Saidie stands and puts herself between me and her friends. "No one's doing anything to anyone. Emma has no reason to out Alex's secret any more than we do to threaten her for something she hasn't done yet. Agreed?"

I shrug. "I was cool until he got all pissy."

"What is this pissy?" Luka still looks scary as all get-out, but he's confused, too. "I have no pissed on anything in here."

Aleric laughs, but he turns away to

hide it.

"Luka takes things very literally," Alex says, her own smile coming out. "His English is getting better, but it still has a long way to go. She meant you're acting like a baby."

He frowns, not liking that any better. "I am no. I am protecting you, Alexandria."

"Look, can we move past the show of testosterone? Kristoff is very much a threat we do need to worry about."

"Agreed." Aleric nods approvingly.

"I need to get him out of the way so I can focus on finding my friend."

"You have a friend missing?"

I sink back down on the bed, miserable as thoughts of what Kane's going through once again take up every corner of my mind. "He's a reaper. He was assigned to teach me how to control my powers, but he was more than that. He's family. He protected me from his bosses when they wanted to kill me. He got into trouble because of me. He helped me with things non-reaping related, and they used that to punish him. They have him somewhere, and I don't know where. I have to be able to get out of this house so I can hunt for him. That new reaper lady made it sound like they're hurting him."

"That's awful," Alex says softly, her blue eyes wide with concern.

"I don't know where he is or if I can even get there to rescue him since my body is very much human. I've checked with the Historians I know, and they have no clue where they take errant reapers."

"I'll ask my mom. She knows a lot more about this kind of stuff than we do. Maybe she or Uncle Sabien can help."

Normally, I'd tell her no simply because her mom made me so mad I seriously thought about throwing her out of the house, but this is for Kane. I can deal with her for his sake.

"I'd appreciate anything you can do." Another thought occurs. "Can I ask you a question?"

She nods.

"I don't know a lot about shifters, but your mom seemed to, I don't know...sniff the air and get a little territorial downstairs earlier? It was weird."

Alex sighs. "Weird isn't the right word, but let me ask you a question first. How is it you don't know a lot about shifters if you're a shifter?"

"Ah, well, I tend to absorb the powers of the people around me, and when I faced down a shifter bar Cass drug us to, I sort of gained their abilities, I think."

"Have you shifted?"

I shake my head.

"Huh. It took me a long time to shift, too. Someone put a wall up around my shifting ability. It almost killed me the first time I tried."

"I have a wall up around most of the protections I inherited from my mother, protections that would keep my human body safe, and all we know is that it was done when I was little. We don't know why, and no one can access the locked door."

"Maybe while we're here, we can see if you can shift or if you just absorbed the abilities of the shifters," Alex muses. "Though, to be fair, shifting is epic. Painful, but once it's done, there's nothing like it. It's…it's indescribable."

"So, about what happened down there with your mom…"

"Now I understand why she's not pitching a fit over my dad marrying my step-mother, who's name happens to be Emma."

"Get out!"

"No, it's really Emma. I guess our worlds are colliding in more ways than one."

"What do you mean?"

"I recognized what happened earlier, but I don't think you're going to like it, considering your feelings about my mother."

That sounds ominous.

"You know wolves mate for life, yeah?"

No, but I don't acknowledge that. "Sure."

"Shifters are the same. When we meet our mate, our senses come alive. Their scent invades us, and it's all we can concentrate on. That's what happened—my mom met her mate."

"Who?"

"Your father."

"Uh…no. He has a girlfriend he loves very much, someone who's important to him."

"That may be, but there's no running from a mate bond, not even for the human who happens to be said mate."

No, no, no, no, no.

No.

"Fudgepops," I whisper. Zeke would never hurt Nancy like that. He wouldn't.

"He doesn't have to choose her," Alex says quietly. "He can walk away from it, but for a shifter, we can't. My mother will never move past it, even if your father does."

"I…I need to go talk to my dad."

Getting up, I go for the door, not even bothering to say goodbye to the people inside.

The only thought on my mind is Nancy.

Saidie

"What do we think?" Alex asks after Emma runs like a woman possessed out of the room, slamming the door behind her.

"She's not who I thought she'd be." I was dead wrong about that girl.

"Who did you expect, *draga*?" Aleric quirks a brow.

"A spoiled rich kid, not a girl who grew up fending for herself in foster care and seems to be as loyal to the people she loves as we are to each other. She's a fighter."

"No." Aleric laces his fingers with

mine. "She's a survivor."

"I no like her," Luka declares. "She's arrogant."

"And you're not?" Alex teases him.

Luka glares at her, and she only laughs. "I like her, but I'm not so sure I like how we all opened up to her. It's like I couldn't *not* tell her what she wanted to know, if that makes sense."

Alex is right. Whenever Emma asked a direct question, I found myself blurting out the truth. "Did you sense any kind of magic?"

"No. Whatever it was, it wasn't magic."

"She cou' taste de truth on us." Aleric's fingers tighten around mine. "Almost like a vampire can."

"She did say she absorbs the power of those around her," I point out. "Kinda like you, Alex."

"Maybe."

Alex is a Cyphon as well as an Elementalist, something we keep hidden from everyone outside our circle. She and her brother have a contract on their heads already. No need to add more money, which would renew efforts to collect the bounty.

That whole Alesha mate thing has thrown both Alex and her brother Jason for a loop. Neither of them looks happy about it. Alex and Jason have been trying to rebuild a relationship with Alesha, and if she moves to New Orleans to be close to Ezekiel, I'm not sure that will ever happen. And I'm not sure that's a bad thing either. As much as I'm grateful to Alesha for all she's done for me personally, I get that what she did to her kids was wrong. It's something that will stay with them forever, so I don't know if it's possible for them to forgive her, let alone give her another chance.

Why is life so complicated the older we get?

"Maybe we can earn some goodwill from her and the people here. Do you think your uncle knows anything about where reapers might take one of their own if they're being punished?"

She shrugs. "No clue."

I pull out my phone and text Sabien to come to my room. Since he's right down the hall, it only takes a minute or two for him to knock on the door.

Sabien Blackburne is the spitting image of his niece. She doesn't look like her mother at all, and Jason is a mini version of his father aside from the Blackburne signature blue eyes. Alex, however, could be Sabien's daughter instead of his niece.

"What's going on? Is something wrong?" He steps inside, and I close the door behind him.

"No, but we're hoping you can help us with something."

He takes note of Alex wrapped up in Luka's arms, holding on so tightly she'd hurt a regular person. "Alex?"

"I'm fine, Uncle Sabien. Promise."

He doesn't believe her any more than I do. Talking about that other reality she'd been trapped is hard on her. Deep down, I think she believes she left the real world behind and chose the reality her mind made up to help her get through what happened to her.

"What do you know about reapers?"

"Not a lot. Why?"

"Emma came and introduced herself, and we got to talking. She's a living reaper."

Sabien nods. "I know."

Of course he does.

"Anyway, she had a teacher who was her friend, and he got taken away from her and punished. She wants to rescue him but has no idea where they're keeping him. We were hoping you might be able to shed some light on it."

"Unfortunately, no, but I think I might know someone who can. I'll need a few hours to make some calls."

"I think if we can help her rescue her friend, it'll go a long way in getting her to trust us. She puts as much stock in family loyalty as we do."

"And she considers this reaper family?"

"Yes."

"I'll see what I can do. Is there anything else you need?"

"Nah, we're all good."

"I'm going to bed, then. I suggest you children do the same. Tomorrow will be a long day."

"What's tomorrow?"

"We're going to sit down with the hunters and try to come up with an action plan to get those things out of the water so Alesha and I can figure a way to unspell them."

"Dey be called crawlers." Aleric shivers, and I hug him.

"Do you know what kind of spell Madame used on them?"

He shakes his head. "She already had dem when I went to live dere."

"We'll figure it out."

Once Sabien's gone back to his room, I push Aleric into a chair and settle in his lap. I can feel his heartbeat flying out of control. His fear of the crawlers is deeper than mine. "You're safe," I whisper. "They can't get you."

His jaw clenches, and I want nothing more than to murder Madame all over again. I don't call women bitches often, but she deserves that title and more. I hate her.

"Have you figured out what you want to do with all her stuff?" Alex nuzzles Luka's neck. He still looks irritated.

"I don't want any of it."

"Uncle Sabien says she has millions of dollars that's now yours. I think you should keep the money as payment for all the things she put you through. You earned that money, Saidie."

"It's blood money, Alex. Who knows who she killed to get it?"

"And maybe she was really good at the stock market. All I'm saying is that if she were a doctor, you'd sue her for malpractice, and a court would award you that money for pain and suffering. You and Aleric deserve a life, and that money can make sure you get it. Sell off the property or give it away or burn it to the ground, but keep the money."

"I'll think about it."

"Good. Now go to bed. Uncle Sabien's right. We all need to get some sleep."

"It's not even ten o'clock."

She stares me down, and I laugh. "Girl, you are not going to sleep. You just want me out of this room to get that one naked."

"Like you're not going to be doing the same thing."

"You know it."

The boys laugh, and Aleric stands with me in his arms. "Come, *draga*, let's get you naked."

And for the rest of the night, our plans are to forget about everything.

Emma

Zeke wouldn't even answer me when I banged on his door, and I went back upstairs, feeling helpless. I hate that he's in there torturing himself for a choice that was taken out of his hands. He likes Cass—respects him, even—and to find out the boy is his son...I can't even imagine what he's going through.

Our talk about this mate bond thing is going to have to wait.

Pulling out my phone, I text Dan to tell him to stay safe and I love him. He sends me one back almost immediately saying pretty much the same thing. I hope he's not taking chances. He's hurt. Knowing Dan, though, he'll jump headfirst into trouble if it means saving someone. It's part of the Dan Richards charm.

Not in the mood to do much of anything, I wander into the kitchen looking for food. I didn't eat dinner, and now my stomach is reminding me in full Mattie Hathaway fashion. It's so loud, it could wake all the people in China.

My dad's housekeeper, Mrs. Banks, made some kind of fancy roast for dinner, but I'm not in the mood for that, so I dig around until I find a container of homemade mac and cheese. She promised to show me how to make the sauce. I'm a mac and cheese connoisseur. Aside from a cheeseburger, it's my favorite food in the entire world. After heating it in the microwave, I shove a forkful into my mouth and just about die from sheer bliss. There's nothing better than yummy, gooey cheese.

My phone rings, and I glance at it. Unknown number. Huh. Letting it go to voicemail, I scarf down more mac and cheese. I hope to God I can learn to make this without burning the house down. I could live off this and a good burger for the rest of my life. I might get fat, but it'll be worth it.

The same number interrupts my meal again, and this time I answer it, afraid they'll just keep calling. If it's telemarketers, I know exactly how to handle those vultures.

"Hello?"

"Emma."

My hand starts to shake.

"You haven't been playing our game, and I'm starting to get a little irritated."

Kristoff.

"I think your message was delivered loud and clear when you sent that bomb to Dan's apartment." At least I don't sound like I'm sitting here shaking. There are very few things that have ever scared me—Dan dying, Silas, and Kristoff. Well, I can add that Romani guy to the list. He's as scary as Silas and Kristoff all rolled into one.

"I wish I could take credit for it, but I cannot. Someone else is responsible for that. I would never do anything to cause your death until I'm ready for you to die."

I knew that didn't smell like Kristoff.

"What do you want?"

"I want to play, Emma. That was our arrangement, or don't you remember? We'd play our game of cat and mouse, and the people you cared about would stay safe, but you're not playing."

"I'm not *not* playing."

"You're drinking dead man's blood to keep me out of your dreams."

"If I make it easy, where would the fun be in that? You'd lose interest."

He laughs. It's a rich, deep sound. Pleasant, really, and if I didn't know I was talking to a madman, it'd be a nice laugh.

"I like you, Emma Crane, and that's why I'm giving you this one chance or someone you love will pay for your disobedience."

My phone dings, and I pull it away to see a text from the unknown number. A picture of Mary's mom at work shows up when I open it. It's dated and time coded. It was taken just a few minutes ago.

Fudgepops.

"Come out and play, Emma, or she's the first who'll pay for your rule-breaking."

"What do you want me to do?"

I don't have to see him to know he's grinning from ear to ear. Sick, twisted psychopath.

"I have a car waiting for you. Get yourself to the main road. You have ten minutes, or your foster mother pays the price of your insubordination. And, Emma, don't tell anyone what you're doing. Leave your phone at home." He disconnects the call.

Crap.

I don't even think. I just get up and go out the kitchen door. I know him well enough to know he'll hurt Mrs. Cross. I can't let anything happen to Mary's mom. She took me in and gave me a home, accepting me and my ability to see ghosts. I'm not going to be responsible for letting him hurt her.

I run through the gardens and scale the back wall. It's easy. Zeke has too many trees close to the walls. I was always climbing and breaking into buildings growing up. This is a piece of cake compared to some of the places I've breached.

Just like he said, I find an old Toyota Corolla parked just out of view of the security cameras. Getting in the driver's side, I see a note taped to a GPS.

Follow the directions, and I'll see you soon.

Starting the car, I wait for the GPS to come on and find only one address programmed into it.

And it's not even in New Orleans.

Heck, it's not even in Louisiana.

A shrill ringing startles me, and I see a burner phone laying on the seat. I answer it.

"Good girl. Someone will call you when it's time to stop for gas. There's an envelope of cash in the glovebox. Once you arrive, you and I are going to play, Emma Crane. I really hope you survive it."

Four hours later, the phone rings, and a man tells me to take a right. An all-night gas station comes into view. It's old school with no cameras. I fill up the tank and go inside, buying a Coke and a bag of chips. I'm starving, and my nerves are making it worse.

I get back on the road and see I have seven more hours to go before I reach my destination in Missouri. I shut everything off inside, blocking Dan and even Silas. I don't want to endanger them until I figure out what Kristoff is playing at. I'm not worried about Silas's safety, but if he tries to rescue me, it could cost Mrs. C her life, and I won't risk it.

Night bleeds into daylight as I drive, my mind numb. I turn the radio on just for the noise. I stop and get gas again, this time grabbing a breakfast biscuit the run-down gas station sells. Again, there are no cameras here. Kristoff is making sure no one can track me. He's as smart as I gave him credit for.

I yawn, turning the car down a long road that was probably very well taken care of but is now more dirt and cracked asphalt than road. A very large stone wall comes into view, the cast iron gate as imposing now as it was when this place was open.

My headlights hit on the dilapidated sign.

Fullson's Sanitarium.

It's an abandoned hospital for the insane.

He brought me to a nuthouse where they housed just not the ordinary, run-of-the-mill nutsos, but the criminally insane as well. The sign says so. There are dangerous ghosts here. He knows I'm a reaper. He knows I can see them, feel them.

Not just that, though. I'm like a lighthouse in a storm to ghosts. They flock to me without ever understanding why, and that can cause confusion, hostility, and rage. These ghosts could do me serious harm.

My phone rings, and the same man who's been giving me directions is on the other end of the line, telling me to pull around to the back. I follow his instructions, doing my best to ignore the ghosts staring at me, some disfigured, others as normal as I am, but with a crazed look about them. Back in the day, there were plenty of people who got put into these places who didn't deserve to be here, but there are just as many who did. They're the ones you have to watch out for.

I park the car and get out, going up to the back door and pushing it open. The stink is almost unbearable. It smells like urine and decay. Who knows how many countless vagabonds have used this place since it closed? I'm not even sure when it closed, as I'm not familiar with the place, but the trash, dirt, and general state of disrepair are a big clue that it was a very long time ago.

A man is standing in the room directly across from me. He's wearing dark slacks, a green dress shirt, and glasses. Normal. I'd never even look at him twice on the street until he got close enough for me to smell.

He smells like rot. He's not a vampire, and he's not dead. But he's not quite human, either.

"What are you?"

"A ghoul."

No clue what that is.

He motions for me to follow him. "My name is Ralph, and you'll see me during the day. I'll bring you food and water, and if you need the facilities, I will take you there as well."

He expects me to just follow along like an obedient puppy? He so does not know me.

Ralph pulls out his phone and taps a few times then turns it to me. There's a live video feed of Mrs. C asleep in her bed. He taps it again, and it changes to Nancy at work.

"This is why you're going to do as you're told. If you don't, they suffer. Do we understand each other?"

I nod. I want to tear him to pieces, but I can't risk Nancy or Mrs. C getting hurt, and Kristoff is banking on my protective instincts.

"Now, come along." Ralph sets off again, this time turning down a hallway and then down a set of stairs.

The basement.

Of course it would be the freaking basement.

He flips a switch at the bottom of the

stairs, and dim light flickers to life. We go through two more hallways and down another flight of stairs, deeper into the abyss.

The worst of the ghosts are down here. I can see their disfigured faces leering at us. They were experimented on, the awful wounds inflicted on them in life permanently etched into their visage in death.

"Be careful."

Ralph stops and turns to look at me.

"The ghosts down here are truly insane. They want to hurt us."

"They have no power over me." He starts walking again, and the ghosts become agitated.

"You think just because you ingested Kristoff's blood that will keep you safe from the ghosts here?"

"Yes."

"You're wrong." The wails of the deranged rise in agreement. "I'm a reaper. Ghosts are my business, and trust me when I say they will eat you alive."

He shrugs. "I'm not going to be here long, anyway."

We stop a few minutes later in front of a heavy iron door that looks medieval. "In you go."

Inside, there's a single mattress on the floor, a sink, and a lone lightbulb that doesn't even chase the shadows from the corners of the room.

"You'll find warmer clothing in that box over there as well as sheets and a blanket. This is Missouri, not Louisiana. It gets cold here."

He pulls something from his pocket. "Come here."

"What is that?" The heavy black leather band sits like a threat in his hands.

"I'm not going to hurt you. I have no desire to see you hurt at all. I'm simply following orders."

"Tell me what that is."

"It's a tracker. A way for me to make sure you're not trying to escape."

"It looks like a collar."

"That's because it is." He motions for me to come to him, and I can't help it. I balk. I don't want that thing on me. Bad memories are associated with it.

"No."

"Don't make me call my associates to hurt one of those nice ladies, Emma."

"You don't understand…"

"But I do understand. I was the one who researched Mattie Hathaway. I know exactly what this collar means to you."

"You're as sick and twisted as he is."

He smiles like he's chatting about the weather. "Why do you think he chose me? Now, come over here before I have to make a call."

I can do this. For Mrs. C and Nancy, I can do this.

Forcing one foot in front of the other, I go to stand in front of him. He reaches up and pushes my hair over one shoulder, his fingers caressing my throat.

He brings the collar up and pulls it tight, so tight it almost cuts off my air. It's right there on the verge of choking me, and I can only take small, shallow breaths.

Ralph says a few words, and the air around us heats and sizzles, snaps with electricity, and the collar eats into my flesh, burning it as it settles in place.

Instinctively, my hands reach up and

try to pull it away, but it's fused into my flesh. It's hugging my windpipe, and there is no escaping it.

"See, that wasn't so bad, now, was it?" Ralph asks, his smile back in place. "A few things. This room is made of iron. Considering how much ghost energy you have, my master has insulated the floor so you can stand. I wouldn't advise touching the walls. They'll burn you. The room is impenetrable to magic. Even the strongest locator spell won't be able to penetrate this room, so don't hold out hope anyone will find you. There's enough food and water over there for at least three days. I'll be back when they run out. Kristoff should arrive tomorrow night, and your games will begin."

He turns to go, but he stops at the door. "The collar you're wearing prevents you from using your magic. You won't even be able to see the ghosts around you," that creepy smile is back, "so I'd advise trying to stay as still and quiet as you can. It's dangerous down here."

He closes the door behind him, and I hear several locks click into place.

Leaving me all alone in an insane asylum full of ghosts I can't see anymore.

Saidie

Bedlam erupts just as Aleric and I are getting out of the shower. Shouting and running footsteps can be heard downstairs, and we both hurry to get dressed to go see what's going on.

Ezekiel is standing in the middle of the front entryway with two phones, shouting into them both. His face is pale, but he's furious. Scared and enraged. Something bad must have happened.

Alex rounds the corner and sees me, relieved. I rush to her, stopping short of touching her. "What happened?"

"Emma's gone."

"Gone? What do you mean, gone?"

"Missing. Her phone and her car are here, but she's not."

"We were just talking to her."

Her lips thin, but other than that, she doesn't say anything else. We move out of the way as the two guys from earlier barrel into the room, an iPad clutched in the hand of the one who has the build of a football player.

"Zeke, she jumped the back fence, and we lost sight of her when she walked past the security cameras in the front."

"Did she get into a car?"

"We listened, but we don't hear one. She could have walked farther up the road where the cameras wouldn't have picked up on the sound."

"What the hell is she doing? She knows better than this. Why did she leave her phone?"

"I'm guessing she didn't have a choice," the other one says. "There's an unknown number on her phone, and it's blocked, so I can't even call it back. Kristoff called and threatened her."

"But how? We have all of you covered,

and Dan is surrounded by police."

"We don't have everyone covered." The guy does something to the phone and shows him a photo. "I didn't tell Mary. She'd freak out if she knew a picture of her mom was texted to Mattie."

Mattie? Who the heck is Mattie?

"That's the only reason Hathaway would have left the house—if someone she loves was threatened. You know that, Zeke."

Her father lets out a string of curse words and slams his hand through the window he's standing beside.

"Shit," I mutter and run over to him. I know first aid, thanks to my mom. Aleric hands me his shirt, and I grab at Ezekiel before thinking. He growls, and Aleric moves me out of the way before I get hit. Shock registers when he realizes what he almost did.

"I'm so sorry." He runs a hand through his hair, and blood drips down his face from the cuts freely bleeding on said hand.

"I just want to help. Your hand needs taken care of."

He looks at his hand dripping blood onto the hardwood floor, blinking like an owl.

"What…"

"You put your hand through the window," Alesha explains and takes the shirt from me, gently wrapping it around his hand.

"Get away from him."

We all turn to see a man with black eyes stalking forward. The smell of sulphur clogs the air, and Alesha throws her magic at him. It bounces off like it hits an invisible shield. He rips her hands away from Ezekiel and snarls. "Do you think I'd let a witch get the blood of my family?"

"I…" She stares wide-eyed at Zeke, who is staring at the man with just as much shock as Alesha.

"Boy, get me water."

The non-football guy goes running. He's back with two bottles of water, which he dumps over Alesha's hands held captive by the British-speaking man.

"That's all of it, Silas. You can let her go now."

Silas drops her hands and turns to survey the scene. He clucks, and just like that, all the blood on the floor and on the broken window disappears, as well as Ezekiel's wounds. His hands are back to normal. "I thought I taught you better than to let a witch get a hold of your blood."

"I was trying to help him."

"Touch him again, and you won't live to take your next breath."

Shit. I take a step back, as does everyone else in the room, including those familiar with him. He's right up there with Kristoff scary, and that's saying a lot.

"I know what you are," Alesha says, her expression morphing into one of disgust. "Touch me, and you'll die."

Instantly, she's thrown up into the air and slammed against the wall, screaming. The flesh is tearing from her body one strip at a time, and the guy…thing…whatever he is isn't even touching her.

"I warned you, witch."

"Silas." Ezekiel puts his hand on the

man's shoulder. "She's here to help. We need her to find Emma."

I've seen the slow-motion effect in movies, but never in real life. Silas's head swivels a centimeter at a time until he's looking at Ezekiel. And all the while, Alesha's flesh is still peeling away from her body, her screams bringing everyone downstairs.

Sabien doesn't run. He doesn't rush. He walks downstairs, assessing.

Or so I thought. He's muttering a spell, but one he doesn't get to complete because his mouth disappears, and he's tossed up onto the wall beside his sister. Thankfully, there is no flesh ripping going on.

"Where is my granddaughter, Ezekiel?"

Emma is his granddaughter?

"Don't," I hear Bree whisper, and I see Jason staring at his mother. He may not like her very much, but he loves her. Seeing her like this has to be more than he can take. "That thing's a demon. He'll kill you as soon as look at you."

He's a demon *and* he's Emma's

grandfather? What the hell did we get ourselves into?

"She's gone. She climbed the back wall, and we don't know where she went."

"That girl…all she had to do was call me. Have you done a locator spell?"

"That's what Alesha was attempting to do when you did that." Ezekiel tosses his hand toward Alesha, no more concerned about her than Silas. Shit. He doesn't care about her at all. "It's why I called you. Emma said you put a tracking spell on her and you could find her anywhere."

"I did, but it's not working."

"You haven't…"

"I started tracking the second you said she was gone. It's not working. Wherever she is, I can't find her."

Ezekiel's knees give out, and he hits the floor, a strange keening noise coming out of him. "Not again. I can't lose her again."

"Call the Willow boy. Get him here. I know of a spell, but it needs his blood to work. Where's Nathaniel?"

"He's out driving, looking for her."

"Boy…"

"Ethan, my name's Ethan."

"Boy, call him and get him here. I'll be back. I need to go collect supplies."

"Wait!" Ethan shouts as Silas starts to shimmer.

"What?"

He gestures to Alesha and Sabien.

Silas flicks his hands, and there's a thud when the two of them drop to the floor. There's not an ounce of flesh out of place on Alesha's face, but she's still screaming. Alex and Jason rush over to them, making sure they're not hurt.

When I look back, the demon is gone.

Bree's eyes are wide, and she hasn't moved from her spot on the stairs. Conner and Micah are behind her, both of them as stunned as we are.

"Help us get them to their rooms," Alex says, and we all help her and her brother carry Alesha and Sabien upstairs, leaving the hot mess downstairs alone.

"We need to leave," Bree says. "My family does a lot, but we don't deal with demons or families who have lain with demons."

"We can't leave." Conner has that faraway look in his eyes, a sure sign he's having a vision.

"Yeah, Conner, we can," Bree argues. "You've never dealt with demons."

"If we leave, she'll die."

"What do you mean?"

"They need us here. If we can find Kristoff before he kills her, we can save her, but if we leave, she's dead. No one will be here to deal with the things in the swamp. More people will die. Without Kristoff to rein them in, they'll go on a killing spree, pulling the focus away from Emma and to them. She'll die."

"That's on them. I'm not staying anywhere with people who will breed with demons."

Jason comes over. "You'd really leave people to die?"

"She's not my concern. You and the people in this room are."

"But her father is my mother's mate."

Bree stubbornly shakes her head.

Jason steps away from her. "I'll have someone find you a ride to the airport in the morning. None of the rest of us are leaving someone to die."

"Jason."

He shakes his head. "No. I never knew you were so cold, so callous. I don't know if it's because you grew up in this world, but I'm glad my sister and I didn't. I'm glad we were raised to care about others and to help where we can. I'm sorry, Bree."

"What are you saying?"

"I think it's best if we don't see each other anymore."

She gasps. "Jason…"

He holds his hand up to stop whatever she's about to say. "You're not my mate, Sabrina."

She looks like he just slapped her, and in a way, I guess he did. She's devastated. "Just go back to your room. I'll talk to that butler guy about arranging transportation back to the airport for you."

Without another word, she walks out, slamming the door behind her.

"So, what now?" Micah asks.

"Now, we wait. Make sure these two are okay and give them time to calm down downstairs. We're not doing anyone any good getting in the way. Once day breaks, we'll be able to do more."

Day breaks with still no sign of Emma. The Willow boy, as Cass Willow was referred to, texted that he'd get her as soon as he could. He was on a hunt two states over. Alesha is still unconscious, but Sabien's up. He hasn't left her side. Alex and Jason let him take over as soon as he was able. They love their mother, but at the same time, it's hard for them to show that love.

We all trudge downstairs a little after six in the morning. I need coffee to function, and if we're going to help them get Emma back, the java must be flowing.

Yawning, I walk like a true zombie to

the kitchen. Jason found it last night when he came downstairs for something to drink. A middle-aged woman is standing by the stove, dishing eggs out of a frying pan and into a serving dish. Her light brown hair is pulled up into a ponytail, and she's wearing jeans and a sweatshirt. Not the kind of uniform I'd expect in this rich place.

"Good morning." She smiles. "I'm Mrs. Banks, housekeeper and cook. I just finished setting up the breakfast buffet in the dining room. Most everyone is in there, if you want to follow Jameson. He's taking the last of the eggs in for me."

She looks tired. There are dark circles under her eyes. She's probably worried about Emma. People seem to love her a lot, which says more about her than anything I could learn by talking to her.

Jameson motions for us to follow him, and I let my nose lead me to the smell of fresh brewed coffee. Ezekiel is sitting at the formal dining table with two women I don't know. Ethan and his friend as well as the blonde girl are there. Food is set out on the buffet behind them, and I get an eerie sense of déjà vu.

My first morning at Madame's, she had a spread set up like this. It's where she introduced me to my first human zombie, the one with its soul trapped inside, who Kristoff was torturing.

Aleric squeezes my hand. He remembers, too.

Conversation stops when we enter, and we sort of stand there awkwardly until the woman sitting next to Zeke smiles. "Good morning. I'm Nancy. You must be hungry. Please help yourselves to coffee and food."

She's beautiful with her mocha skin and dark brown eyes. Warmth oozes out of her. And when Ezekiel looks at her, it's with such love and affection, I understand why he ignored Alesha last night. Why her pain meant nothing to him. He's looking at her the way Aleric looks at me. This woman owns his heart.

"You'll have to forgive me. I'm just getting a crash course in all things supernatural this morning."

Now, how the hell is that possible? She

can't be dating Ezekiel Crane and not know about his world. Or maybe she doesn't, or didn't. If I could spare the people I love from knowing about it, I probably would, too.

"Has anyone heard from Dan yet?" the blonde asks as she pushes food around on the plate in front of her. "I've texted and left more voicemails than I can count. Are we sure he's safe?"

"He and his team are out at a crime scene where there's no cell service. That's all I got." Ethan yawns, and the guy sitting beside him hands him a coffee cup. "Eric, I do not like as much sugar as you dump in your coffee."

"I made it the way you like it. Now, stop being surly and drink it."

He flashes Eric a grateful smile, and I get the whole boyfriend vibe from them, but again, I don't know them well enough to make assumptions.

We all help ourselves to coffee and food as suggested. The roast we had last night was delicious, and the pancakes are just as good. I love pancakes. And grits. Oh, my God, they have shrimp and grits.

I think I am in love with Mrs. Banks.

"Sorry for yesterday. It was a bit of a day," blonde girl says. "I'm Mary, and this is my mom, Nadine Cross."

Her mother nods and keeps dialing a number on her phone. "I'm going to get fired, Ezekiel."

"No, you're not, and if you do, I'll get you a job at a hospital down here closer to our girls. They'd love to have you here with us."

"We would, Mom."

She gives her daughter a hesitant smile but keeps her attention on her phone. "No luck. He's still not picking up."

"Who are you trying to call?" I ask.

"Mattie's boyfriend."

"Who's Mattie?"

"Emma. She grew up with the name Mattie Hathaway."

"I knew she looked familiar."

We all turn to see Alesha standing in the doorway with Sabien behind her. She's staring at Nancy, and the wheels are turning in her head. It doesn't take a super sniffer to know these two have to be giving off some serious pheromones.

"What do you mean?" Ezekiel asks.

"I was contacted by a woman named Claire Hathaway to do a memory spell on her daughter. She wanted to keep her safe from someone who she thought might mean to hurt her, and at the same time, she didn't want her to miss them either because the little girl adored him. When she told me it was to keep her safe from a demon, I agreed without hesitation."

"So you're the one who took her memories of Silas away," Mary says. "We won't mention that to him. He's already mad enough as it is. He might kill you where you stand if he knew that."

"My daughter's right," Ezekiel agrees. "Silas would strike you down. We'll keep that to ourselves."

Mrs. Cross glances at him, and he laughs.

"I love Mary like she was my own. I'd give her my last name so she could have all the protections that affords if I thought you'd let me, Nadine."

It's then we hear voices coming down the hallway, and a man walks in. He's dragging, looking ready to pass out on his feet. Cute, though.

"Dan!" Mary jumps up. "Why aren't you answering your phone?"

"It died, and I didn't have a car charger with me. My partner has a Samsung phone instead of an iPhone." His gaze zeroes in on Mrs. Cross, and he straightens, realizing something's wrong. "What's going on?"

"I think you should sit down, Dan." Nancy is up and has her arm wrapped around his. He gently shakes her off.

"No, tell me what's wrong."

"Mattie's missing."

He doesn't react at first, and everyone seems to be holding their breath.

"What do you mean, missing?"

"She left last night when no one was looking."

"No. She wouldn't do that. She knows it's too dangerous."

"They sent her a time-coded photo of Nadine," Ezekiel says. "She left so they wouldn't hurt Mary's mother."

"Silas!" he bellows.

The demon pops in instantly.

"Find her."

"I can't. I've been looking all night. She's dropped off every radar I have set up to track her." The demon's shoulders slump. "She's gone."

"And before you start shouting for Rhea, I've already done that, and she's looking for her, too." Ezekiel stands and grasps his other arm. "Come sit down. You look dead on your feet."

Dan shakes him off, only not as gently as before.

Then something happens.

He seems to grow a good foot in height, and his form gets bigger, thicker. A bluish-white glow surrounds him, and a sword flashes to life on his back, the glow from it stronger and brighter than anything I've ever come across.

Dan pulls the sword and swings it toward Silas, who backs up and puts the table between him and that glowing metal blade. "I thought you said you safeguarded against this happening so the Fallen Angels couldn't get their hands on her again. You're supposed to be able to find her, demon."

"The Fallen didn't take her, Daniel."

Silas keeps his voice low and calm. "Kristoff has her, and he's just as hard to find as she is. He's getting magical help with so much mojo, it's hard to even find a trace of them."

Dan snarls.

"I said hard, not impossible. We're waiting for the Willow boy to get here. I need his blood to find her."

"Why would you need Cass's blood to find her?"

"Because Mattie is unique, and I need demon blood, a living reaper's blood, and angelic blood to find her. The spell calls for those specific things."

Angelic blood, demon blood, and a living reaper's blood. I'm betting her father is the living reaper, and Silas is a demon, so this Cass has to have angelic blood. It's like a soap opera on steroids.

"Dan, put the Sword away," Mary says softly, approaching him as one would a cornered animal, her hands up.

"No."

"Dan, the Sword could hurt someone."

"The Sword judges you. If you have done nothing wrong, it won't harm you."

He swings it toward her, and she stops moving. Everyone stops breathing.

"Dan, the Sword is messing with you. You need to put it down."

His face twists, and his eyes start to glow with that same bluish light surrounding him.

"Dan, there isn't a person alive who hasn't done something they're ashamed of. The Sword doesn't know the difference, but you do. You're going to get one of us killed, and then what would Mattie say? Think, Dan. Just think for a minute. I know you're scared. So are we, but the Sword is feeding off your fear, forcing its will on you. You need to put it down."

I can see the moment when reality breaks through his fog of rage, and the sword falls from his hand. The bright light fades, and he falls, much as her father did last night. Mary carefully picks up the sword and hands it to Eric. Then she goes to her knees beside him. "We're going to find her."

"I can't feel her," he whispers. "I can always feel her, even after Silas blocked most of everything the two of us shared."

"She's not dead," Mary says confidently. "You'd be dead if she were. Take comfort in that."

"She's with a monster, Mary." A single tear slips down his cheek. "He broke her arm, and she let him to keep everyone in the hospital safe. What is she going to let him do to keep us safe?"

"She's a fighter. She survived serial killers, soul eaters, Fallen Angels, blood demons, and everything in between. She'll survive until we can find her."

"She's right." Silas approaches carefully. "I'm going to remove the spell that blocked you from her. You're the only one who might stand of chance of finding her, Daniel."

He looks up, and his eyes have gone to a deep shade of brown so dark they're almost black. Pain lives in them. He's hurting in a way I can't even define.

Silas lays a hand on his forehead, and there's a flash of light, and the stench of sulphur permeates the air. Dan gasps and falls backward, his chest heaving. His hands clutch at his throat, clawing at it like he's choking. He can't breathe, and Mrs. Cross runs over, still wearing her nurse's scrubs. She opens his mouth, checking for an obstruction.

"No, Mom, he's okay. This is what's happening to Mattie. Whatever happens to her happens to him."

"How's that possible if they've cut her off from magic?" Alesha asks curiously.

"Because this isn't magic." Silas frowns. "Her soul is tied to the boy's, and whatever one feels, so does the other. If she dies, he dies, and vice versa. That's why this spell is going to work. Where's the Willow boy?"

"On his way here," Ezekiel says.

"Once we do the spell, we'll need the help of the hunters to find her."

Ezekiel laughs bitterly. "None of them are willing to help. Not even Robert Willow."

Silas's face gets dark with rage. "She has spent the last two years doing everything she can to help them, to make sure they had resources and were paid. She even set up a foundation to help them, and they won't even look for her?"

"Her last name is Crane."

Silas looks at Mary. "Call the boy and tell him what's going on and to get himself here as soon as possible. Until he arrives, all we can do is wait."

"What about Dan?" Mary asks.

"He'll be okay in a few minutes. He's breathing, which means that while it's hard for her to breathe, it's not impossible. As long as she's breathing, he'll continue to. Once he gets used to the limited air, he'll be fine."

Mary gets up and pulls her phone out of her pocket, moving to the side to do as she was told.

I look over at Alex, and she's as freaked out as I am by these people. Angels, demons, and reapers. Oh my.

But the demon's right. All we can do is wait.

Emma

"Bad girl!"

I cower away from the woman and her spatula. She's mad again. I just wanted to color, but it's not time to color yet. Mama always let me color when I wanted to, but Mrs. Harte says we can only color after supper. So I stole the crayons and some paper out of the cabinet. She found me and got so mad.

Her spatula hurts when it hits my bottom. I try to run, but she catches me, and I cry when it smacks me again, catching the backs of my legs. She keeps hitting me, and I bite her to try to get away.

"You ungrateful little beast!" She drags me by the hair down the steps to the basement. "I'll show you how we deal with bad behavior in this house."

In the corner is a single blanket and a chain attached to the wall, a dog collar at the end of it. She throws me onto the blanket and puts the collar around my neck. She uses a small padlock to make sure I can't get it off.

"You'll stay down here until you learn not to sass me."

She goes back up the stairs and turns off the lights, leaving me alone in the dark with the rats.

A sound pulls me out of the nightmare, and I jerk awake. I lie there listening, waiting to hear the sound again, but only silence greets me.

I'm not sure how long I've been down here, but the temperature is frigid. I know it's not just the cold weather, either. I may not be able to see the ghosts, but I can still feel them just outside the door. They can't cross the iron barrier. That's the only thing that's kept me sane. They can't get me in here.

I passed out for a while that first day because I couldn't get enough air into my lungs. I had to get used to it. The pain is still there with every small movement of my head. This collar is eating away at the flesh of my throat, soaking into my muscles. It hurts.

Physically, I can deal with the pain, but mentally? That's a whole other matter. I keep having nightmares about my time in the basement chained to the wall with the rats eating away at my feet and my fingers. I was only seven. It did some serious damage to my psyche, damage that will never go away, and the man who left me here knew it.

So far, no rats have come in the room, but I'm vigilant. I keep the water jug close to brain one should they find a way into my prison. The food's almost gone, but I've been cautious about the water. I don't trust them to not leave me here for days on end without food or water. It's just another sick game they'd play.

I gave in last night and peed in the

corner. My bladder wasn't going to go any longer, and I didn't want to wake up to find I'd peed on myself in my sleep.

Footsteps sound down the hallway, and I tense. Ralph said Kristoff would be here tonight. At least I'm assuming it's been that long. I can't tell.

They stop outside my door, and then I hear the locks turning. When it swings inward, Kristoff steps in. He's wearing jeans and a long-sleeved shirt. His blond hair is spiked artfully, and he looks a little too smug.

"I'm glad you decided to play by the rules, Mathilda Louise Hathaway."

"Ralph did his homework."

"He's very good at it, too. You were quite the little vagrant growing up. I think your rap sheet is longer than Ralph's was at that age."

He leans down and picks up a bag and carries it inside, closing the door behind him. He hands me a Sonic bag and a drink. "I believe you like their bacon cheeseburgers. Don't worry, it's not poisoned or drugged. I want you alert for our little games."

I take the bag and sit down. No point in trying to get around him. He's faster, and he'd only hurt me before he's ready to. And I am hungry. The food is a little cold, but I don't care. It's still food. I scarf it down, and he smiles like a benevolent benefactor.

When he sits across from me, I get tense.

"Our game tonight is going to be a simple one. Truth or dare."

Truth or dare?

"It's unfortunately necessary. I need to make sure you can't escape the other rooms I'm setting up for you and that you can't be found. Which means certain wards and protections must be put in place. There will be no iron in some of them because I want the ghosts to visit you while I sleep, you see."

I clench my fists to keep my hands from shaking. The ghosts down here are more than dangerous. They're deadly.

"This ward we're in is where they housed the most brutal of their patients, the serial killers and those who just enjoyed the scent of blood on their flesh.

They loved the art of killing."

He filches one of my fries and sniffs it. I want to snatch it back, but I refrain.

"I miss food. You don't realize how much until you're lying there and tasting it through your human servant. I want to be able to take a bite of that burger and have the flavor burst across my tongue the same way blood does, but that will never happen."

"Ralph is your human servant?"

He laughs so hard he bends over. "No, Ralph is a ghoul. My human servant is someone else entirely."

"What's a ghoul?"

"They're dead who stay alive by eating human flesh. My blood keeps Ralph's mind whole, and he remains loyal to me because of it."

He looks around and wrinkles his nose. "Ralph was supposed to leave you with something to urinate in."

"Ralph wasn't too big on doing things to help out." I finger the collar at my throat. I need to keep him talking. If he's talking, he's not hurting me.

"The collar was a nice touch. He told

me about the rats."

I shudder; I can't help it.

He grins, enjoying my fear.

"Now, my little mouse, truth or dare?"

"Truth."

"Is it true you can take a beating and heal faster than the average human?"

"No. I don't heal faster than the average human. I can take a hit, though. I grew up learning to take a hit."

My finger is in his hands and bent back before the words leave my mouth. A scream follows when I hear the bone snap.

"Don't lie. Lies will earn you punishments."

"I wasn't," I gasp, trying to breathe through the pain. "I learned to take a hit in foster care."

"You do heal faster than the average human. We've been watching you and talking to people who think you're something to be hunted."

What am I supposed to say to that? I know the hunters are talking. Cass is trying to stop the rumors, but he's just one person. He can't do it all.

"Time for a dare since we started with a truth."

Crap on toast.

"Hmmm…what shall I dare you to do?" His ice blue eyes turn even colder. "Have you ever had someone taste your blood?"

I shake my head.

"A vampire's bite can give great pleasure or great pain. I think I'm going to dare you to let me bite you."

"Let you?"

He nods. "Alice tried to fight me until she realized it was easier to let me feed. Are you going to fight me, Emma Rose?"

"You are not feeding from me." I push away from him, but he's still holding my hand, and he jerks me forward. My body slams into his, and the collar around my throat tightens.

"Beautiful piece of work, isn't it?" He trails his hand over the collar, and I wince as it sinks deeper into my flesh. "It's this collar that's hiding you from everyone. I learned my lesson with Alice. You're hidden, and no one will come looking for you, my sweet girl. You're all mine." His nose traces the outline of my jaw, and when his lips descend on mine, I bite down as hard as I can, ripping flesh in the process.

He backhands me, and I go flying into the wall.

"You're not playing by the rules."

"You never said I couldn't fight you." I shake my head, dizzy.

"I suppose I didn't, but that's why I chose you. You're a fighter. You don't give up." He crooks his fingers and motions for me to come to him.

I know better than to refuse. I crawl over there, unable to stand. My hand is killing me, and I feel the urge to spew all the food I just ate.

"Good girl." He beams. "Now I dare you to hold out your hand and let me feed."

"No."

"That's not how truth or dare works."

"I said no."

"Should we make a call to one of my friends watching those you love?"

"I call BS. As soon as my papa found my phone with Mrs. C's picture on it, he'll have had them brought to the plantation. Everyone I love is safe. Hurt me if you want, but you can't terrorize me with that little threat."

At least I hope I'm right.

"You're spunky. I like that." He reaches out and cradles my head in his hand, his thumb brushing along my lips. "You're a lot spunkier than Alice. She gave out after only a few minutes of our games."

My head hits the cold ground, and pain explodes behind my eyes. He slams it twice more before pulling me into his arms. "Now, hold out your arm and feed me."

"No," I whisper.

He grins, and more pain splinters through my leg as it's crushed in his grip. "The femoral artery is safe. We can't have you bleeding out."

Black spots dance in front of my eyes, and I know I'm close to passing out. I probably have a concussion. I fight the darkness, though. I don't want to be alone with him while I'm out cold.

"You need to rest so I can see how fast

you heal, but I need to eat, too."

He brings my arm to his lips and places the gentlest of kisses on my wrist before he bites down and a new pain starts. It's like acid invading my veins, eating me alive from the inside. I can hear myself screaming as he suckles at my wrist. Pain. All I feel is pain.

When he's done, he lifts me and lays me down on the blanket, setting the water jug beside me. "Sleep, Emma. I'll be back in a few hours, and we'll try this again."

I can't move as he leaves the room, locking the door behind him.

My body is a mess of pain. He's wrong. I can't heal. Silas heals me. My healing abilities are locked away behind a door I can't access. I'm lying here shaking from pain, and all I want is to see Dan, feel him wrap me in his arms and tell me everything's going to be okay. I'm so glad he can't feel any of this. It's the one bright spot in my new sea of darkness.

He's going to put me somewhere the ghosts can get at me. I'm not able to defend myself.

But maybe there is someone who can help.

Closing my eyes, I call for Elsie, my new reaper tutor.

She doesn't come right away. Kane always comes the second I call for him.

I'm not sure how long I lie here before she appears before me, her pixie hair disheveled. She must have been busy.

"What is it?" she demands. "I have souls to collect."

Seriously?

"Elsie, I need your help. I…he's going to let the ghosts in, and he's buried my reaping abilities. I can't…" I wheeze when a new round of pain hits.

"You called me to save you?" She stares at me in amazement. "I'm your teacher in how to be a reaper, not someone to call to rescue you from a situation that has nothing to do with reaping."

"Elsie, please…"

She smiles. "You are not supposed to be here. You're an abomination, and I'm not going to save you."

And then she's gone. It renews my hatred of reapers. Arrogant, soulless creatures. Except for Kane. If I do nothing else, I am going to get out of here so I can save him. I will find a way to sever his ties to them so he can live in peace, reaping but not under the rule of those horrible beings. He deserves better.

Is he hurting like I am? What are they doing to him? Focusing on him instead of the pain in my body helps, but it only lasts for so long. My teeth are chattering. Shock. I'm going into shock. I've been here enough times to recognize it. If I don't get warm, it's going to get worse. Mary's mom taught me how to combat shock because of how often I get injured. Zeke even joked about renting out a hospital room just for me so I always have a bed when I need one. Or I thought he was joking. Truth is, he rented several hospital rooms for his kids, as he calls us.

I miss my papa.

I even miss Lila, who I disappoint on the daily.

None of them know where I am. Kristoff made sure they can't find me.

Even knowing what I know now, I'd still have made the same choice. Mrs. C loves me as much as she does Mary. I will protect her at all costs. My life isn't worth more than hers. If Mary lost her mom, she'd be devastated.

I curl up and whimper as new waves of pain travel up my leg. He crushed the bone. I know Silas could heal me, but he's not here. Wonder what Kristoff will think of his little experiment when he comes back and I'm still in the same shape he left me in?

He might get bored and decide to kill me if I can't entertain him.

That might be the best option, honestly. I'd rather die than suffer more and more pain. I can see the plans he has for me in his eyes. They're hard and cold, but the evil shines through like a bright light.

But if I die, Dan dies. I can't let that happen. I fought too hard to keep him alive. I won't let him die, no matter how much I suffer.

I just need some help.

"Dear God, help me. Please, please

help me."

A feeling I'm familiar with washes over me. Peace and comfort. The pain is still there. I'm still ready to pass out from the head trauma, but I'm not as scared. I can breathe a little more, and I know I'm not alone.

I've never been alone before, and I'm not now. All I had to do was reach out and ask for help, and it's right there. Not in the way most people would demand. The door is still locked, I'm still very badly injured, but I'm okay. I can feel the warmth around me, and I let it lull me into a semi-sleep. I'll rest and take comfort in the fact that I'm going to get through this. I've survived worse than Kristoff, and I'll survive this.

Closing my eyes, I concentrate on the peace and quiet around me. Later will bring more pain and more fear, but for right now, I'm safe and loved. That's what my faith is. It's knowing I can get through anything with God beside me.

"I can't leave you alone for five minutes, can I, Hilda?"

My eyes spring open, and I search the

room, but there's no one there. I really must be out of it.

A pair of sneakers invade my vision, and my gaze climbs ups a pair of jean-clad legs and a green hoodie. Dark blond hair frames a face that smiles all the time, and the most beautiful aqua eyes stare down at me.

My breath hitches. I must be hallucinating. No way is he here.

He squats in front of me and runs a finger over my swollen eye.

"What am I going to do with you, Hilda?"

"Eli?" I whisper, afraid to even breathe his name.

He smiles crookedly at me. "Hey, Hilda."

"You can't be here."

"What did I promise you?"

"That you'd always find me."

"I'm your Guardian Angel, and even death can't break that bond. You asked for help, and here I am."

"Eli?" Tears spring up, and a sob starts deep in my chest.

"Shh, Hilda. Sleep. I'll be here when

you wake up."

He lays a hand on my head, and a deep warmth suffuses my body, forcing me to succumb to the darkness that's been eating away at me.

The Bayou Trilogy will end in *Bayou Reckoning*, coming Spring 2020.

ABOUT THE AUTHOR

So who am I? Well, I'm the crazy girl with an imagination that never shuts up. I LOVE scary movies. My friends laugh at me when I scare myself watching them and tell me to stop watching them, but who doesn't love to get scared? I grew up in a small town nestled in the southern mountains of West Virginia where I spent days roaming around in the woods, climbing trees, and causing general mayhem. Nights I would stay up reading Nancy Drew by flashlight under the covers until my parents yelled at me to go to sleep.

Growing up in a small town, I learned a lot of values and morals, I also learned parents have spies everywhere and there's always someone to tell your mama you were seen kissing a particular boy on a particular day just a little too long. So when you get grounded, what is there left to do? Read! My Aunt Jo gave me my first real romance novel. It was a romance titled "Lord Margrave's

Deception." I remember it fondly. But I also learned I had a deep and abiding love of mysteries and anything paranormal. As I grew up, I started to write just that and would entertain my friends with stories featuring them as main characters.

Now, I live Huntersville, NC where I entertain my niece and nephew and watch the cats get teased by the birds and laugh myself silly when they swoop down and then dive back up just out of reach. The cats start yelling something fierce…lol.

I love books, I love writing books, and I love entertaining people with my silly stories.

SOCIAL MEDIA

Facebook:
https://www.facebook.com/authorAprylBaker

Twitter:
https://twitter.com/AprylBaker

Website:
http://www.aprylbaker.com/

Bookbub:
https://www.bookbub.com/authors/apryl-baker

Wattpad:
http://www.wattpad.com/user/AprylBaker7

Newsletter:
https://www.aprylbaker.com/contact

Facebook Fan Page:
https://www.facebook.com/groups/AprylsAngels

Instagram:
https://www.instagram.com/apryl.baker

Blog:
https://www.mycrazycornerblog.com/

Amazon:
https://goo.gl/b1br13

Join our Reader Group on Facebook and don't miss out on meeting our authors and entering epic giveaways!

Limitless Reading

Where reading a book
is your first step to becoming
limitless...

LIMITLESS ◆ PUBLISHING *Reader Group*

Join today! *"Where reading a book is your first step to becoming limitless..."*